"I bet you won't last one month on this ranch."

"Oh, okay." Miranda laughed. "Some bet there. A whole month. Wow."

"That's all it will take," Jesse said.

"You're really serious? What are we betting?"

"The ranch."

"What?" Miranda rolled her eyes skyward as she shook her head. "What do you mean, the ranch?"

"If you last the month, I'll leave and you'll never be bothered by me again." He grinned. "If I win, you sell me the ranch for what I originally bid on it. What do you say? You game, or don't you think you can handle it?"

Miranda narrowed her eyes. So this was his plan. He still wanted the ranch for himself. Well, one month would be easy enough. And it would teach him a lesson not to underestimate her. There was no way she could lose.

"I've got news for you, cowboy. I'm not going anywhere." Miranda held out her hand. "You have yourself a deal."

Dear Reader,

Family is the glue that keeps us together through the bad times and the confetti in the air during the good times. Family comes in all shapes and sizes and isn't necessarily blood relative exclusive. Ramblewood, Texas, is a small town, big on heart. Where friends and neighbors are a huge part of everyone's family.

I'm excited to share my first book with you. *Betting on Texas* gained momentum while I was sitting around a kitchen table with five other women and two seeing-eye dogs. I can't thank Dorothy, Jan, Lois, Miriam and Pam enough for believing in this book in its infancy. Lois has since passed on, but will always remain a part of my extended family.

When I saw Harlequin's So You Think You Can Write contest, I knew it was time for Miranda and Jesse to see the light of day. Three months later to the day, Senior Editor Kathleen Scheibling made my dreams of becoming an author come true. She has truly become my fairy godmother. And to my fellow American Romance "sisters," thank you for warmly welcoming me into the Harlequin family.

The townsfolk of Ramblewood, Texas, have become a part of my life, just as I hope they become a part of yours. Feel free to stop in and visit me at www.amandarenee.com. I'd love to hear from you. Happy reading!

Amanda Renee

Betting on Texas
AMANDA RENEE

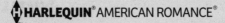

HARLEQUIN® AMERICAN ROMANCE®

If you purchased this book without a cover you should be aware that this book is stolen property. It was reported as "unsold and destroyed" to the publisher, and neither the author nor the publisher has received any payment for this "stripped book."

Recycling programs
for this product may
not exist in your area.

ISBN-13: 978-0-373-75446-5

BETTING ON TEXAS

Copyright © 2013 by Amanda Renee Mayo

All rights reserved. Except for use in any review, the reproduction or utilization of this work in whole or in part in any form by any electronic, mechanical or other means, now known or hereafter invented, including xerography, photocopying and recording, or in any information storage or retrieval system, is forbidden without the written permission of the publisher, Harlequin Enterprises Limited, 225 Duncan Mill Road, Don Mills, Ontario M3B 3K9, Canada.

This is a work of fiction. Names, characters, places and incidents are either the product of the author's imagination or are used fictitiously, and any resemblance to actual persons, living or dead, business establishments, events or locales is entirely coincidental.

This edition published by arrangement with Harlequin Books S.A.

For questions and comments about the quality of this book, please contact us at CustomerService@Harlequin.com.

® and TM are trademarks of Harlequin Enterprises Limited or its corporate affiliates. Trademarks indicated with ® are registered in the United States Patent and Trademark Office, the Canadian Trade Marks Office and in other countries.

Printed in U.S.A.

www.Harlequin.com

ABOUT THE AUTHOR

Born and raised in the northeast, Amanda Renee currently resides on the Intracoastal Waterway in sunny South Carolina. Her dreams came true when she was discovered through Harlequin's So You Think You Can Write contest.

When not creating stories about love, laughter and things that go bump in the night, she enjoys the company of her schnoodle named Duffy, traveling, photography, playing guitar and anything involving horses. You can visit her at www.amandarenee.com.

For my Mom and Dad with love.

And for Grandma Kay—I wish you were here
to share this with me.

Chapter One

Double Trouble. Miranda hoped the words emblazoned across the iron arch at the ranch's entrance weren't an indication of things to come. Well, there was no turning back now. She tossed a crumpled map onto the passenger seat and steered her new black pickup and creaky rental trailer through the gates.

A bittersweet smile formed upon her lips as the house appeared in the distance. This was it. A new home and a new life, away from everything in Washington, D.C.

The morning sun shone bright upon the white clapboards of the century-old farmhouse. A large whitewashed front porch spanned its entire width. Walnut and oak trees shadowed neglected flowerbeds filled with weeds. Miranda envisioned a vibrant wildflower palette planted against the starkness of the house and looked forward to a little garden work.

She pulled the truck into a shaded area close to the stables. Looking up, Miranda's breath caught in her throat. A rough and ready cowboy leaned casually against the weathered open door of the building. A grayish-colored dog sat at his feet, wagging his tail.

If the cowboy comes with the place, I must be in heaven.

Miranda peered over the top of her sunglasses and watched the man walk inside the stables. Then logic overruled fantasy. Miranda realized Jonathan must have arranged for him to welcome her to Ramblewood.

She stepped down from the truck, her body stiff from the long drive. The cowboy returned leading a deep chocolate-brown-colored horse.

Her eyes darted to a nearby corral where two more horses grazed. Coils of rope and feed buckets hung from the white fencing. Water troughs filled to their rims reflected the morning sky. She shook her head, willing the whole scene to disappear.

Something wasn't right.

Miranda grabbed the photos from the front seat. It didn't make sense. It was the same house. Same property. Why were the horses still here?

Maybe he's just using the place for a few days. The horse trailer next to the barn must mean the animals were being relocated soon.

"May I help you?" the man called out as he approached.

His tall, muscular frame flexed with each stride. The Texas sun had tanned his face a warm golden hue. Hair the same color as the horse he led peeked out from under his Stetson. A few days' worth of stubble enhanced his rugged good looks even further.

"Um…" Miranda's mouth went dry. She regained her composure enough to ask, "Is this the Double Trouble Ranch?"

"Sure is, sugar," he drawled. The horse behind him nudged his shoulder forward. "What can I do for you?"

"I don't understand." Miranda surveyed the property.

Are those cows in the distance? She looked to the cowboy for answers. "This has to be a mistake."

His eyes narrowed. Miranda stepped back. The handsome features she was attracted to only seconds ago faded into a menacing glare.

"Who are you?" His jaw clenched.

Miranda had a sudden urge to flee to the safety of her truck, but both man and horse blocked her path. A fierce pounding began deep within her chest. She opened her mouth to speak, but the words wouldn't come.

"You're the new owner, aren't you?"

He stood too close for comfort. Miranda backed into the corral fence. There was no place to turn. With her adrenaline raging, anger suddenly overtook fear. Squaring her shoulders she stepped forward, inches from his face.

"Yes, and you are?"

"The former ranch manager." He handed her the horse's rope. "His name's General Lee. Good luck."

Stunned, Miranda looked up at the animal. He snorted and licked her cheek. "Eww!" She wiped her face and quickly lengthened the amount of rope between herself and the horse.

"Hey, wait a minute," Miranda called out after the cowboy who was walking away. The sound of hooves on the ground behind her stopped her—she forgot all about the rope she held. The horse nudged her forward. "Cut that out!"

The cowboy stopped in front of Miranda's truck and looked down at the bug-splattered license plate.

"Washington, D.C., huh? What's a city girl like you know about owning a ranch?"

"Nothing!" she shouted. At her outburst General Lee

tossed his head pulling the rope through Miranda's hand with a stinging burn.

The cowboy was back at the agitated horse's side, rubbing his palm between the horse's eyes and down to the end of his muzzle while he whispered words Miranda couldn't quite make out.

"Lesson one. Don't ever yell around a horse. Especially one you don't know," he warned. "Lesson two—always wear gloves when handling a rope."

"But—" There was no point in reminding him he was the one who'd handed it to her. She closed her eyes tight. *It's all a dream. The Marlboro Man is just a mirage.*

"I don't understand. I bought this place but…I didn't sign on for this." She gestured toward the horse. "Why are you here?"

"I wanted to meet the person who destroyed my life." He stepped closer.

Didn't this man understand the meaning of personal space? He stared at her with deep brown eyes as if he expected an explanation. He may be drop-dead gorgeous, but she wasn't about to let him intimidate her. Yes, he was an incredible specimen of a man, but she needed to focus on the task at hand.

If only I could run my hands—

Miranda shook her head to erase the thought, watching the cowboy turn General Lee loose within the fenced area. The cowboy returned and gave her a conceited grin, as if he'd read her mind.

"You outbid me," he said.

"What are you talking about?"

"I know your type." He drew her hands to his chest and ran his thumbs over her skin. "Rich as molasses.

Everything in life handed to you on a silver platter. You come to these small Texas towns, buy ranches like this one and then turn them into housing developments."

He turned her palm upward while gingerly running his fingers over the welt from the rope. A chill ran through her. A part of her wanted him far away from her yet she seemed to be glued to the spot. Maybe it had been far too long since she last felt the touch of a man. But this wasn't just any man—this was a full-blooded cowboy who rattled her as no one ever had.

The reality of the situation kicked in and she pushed him away. "Not that it's any business of yours, but I bought this place to live on. Sight unseen, I might add. I don't know where you got your information from, but it couldn't be more wrong. I have no plans to build anything. I don't have that kind of money."

"Sure you don't." He ground his teeth together. "I poured the past fifteen years of my life into this ranch. Built everything you see here, with the exception of the houses. Double Trouble was mine. Then you came along. Ripped it right out from under me. Too bad I won't be around to watch when you try to deal with the cattle."

"Cattle?" Miranda gulped. So, those were cows in the distance.

My cattle!

"Those things out there with the big horns are called Longhorns. And they're all yours." He laughed. "Don't fret too much. It's only a small herd used for training the cutting horses."

"Look…mister…whatever your name is."

"Jesse," he interrupted.

"Look, Mr. Jesse, I don't know what's going on

around here. There must be some mistake. I thought the sale included whatever contents the owners left behind in the house. I figured it meant furniture. It never crossed my mind livestock would come with the property and I never thought to ask. I don't know how to take care of them."

Miranda ran over the events of the past month in her mind. Her ex-fiancé's lack of sympathy regarding her mother's death made her decision to move that much easier. When Jonathan Reese, her lawyer and best friend since eleventh grade, returned from Texas and told her he found the perfect place for her to start over, she found the opportunity impossible to resist. Memories of countless moves and dingy, cramped apartments led way to dreams filled with wide-open spaces and a farmhouse in the country.

Now she owned her dream. And while she may have seen an animal or two in the photographs, no one ever told her it was a package deal.

A rooster crowed and broke her train of thought. "Chickens, too?"

"You're telling me you know nothing about horses and cattle? Then why on earth did you buy a ranch?"

"I just told you, I didn't know it came complete with farm animals. I bought a house with land."

"Lady, this is a ranch! And ranches are for people with animals."

Miranda kicked at the dirt beneath her boots. She needed a moment to sort this out, to call Jonathan and get to the bottom of this.

"What did you intend to do with a fifteen stall stable?"

"There are fifteen horses?" If she didn't faint now, she would soon.

"Relax." Jesse smirked. "There's not quite that many now. So what happened? The truck wasn't expensive enough for you? Had to jump in whole hog and buy a Texas ranch to appease your shopping urges?"

Miranda's first thought was to slap him across the face. Thank heavens her good graces held her in check and she kept her hands where they were.

"Oh, get off your high horse. No pun intended there, cowboy." Miranda recoiled. "You know nothing about me!"

"Don't care to, either."

"If you are so concerned about the welfare of these animals, then why don't you take them with you?"

"And keep them where? My back pocket? Not a whole lot of room there, sugar."

Miranda ignored his arrogance. "Mr. Jesse, certainly there must be some room for them at your ranch."

"You sure don't listen very well. This *was* my ranch!" Lines of frustration creased his forehead. "And my name's Jesse Langtry, not Mr. Jesse."

"Jesse's your first name?" Miranda tried to hide her amusement. "Like Jesse James?"

"You got a problem with that, city slicker?" He folded his arms across his chest.

"City slicker!" Miranda found it harder and harder to keep calm. "Look, it's obvious there's been some sort of a mix-up here. Once I call my attorney, I'm sure I can straighten this all out. Maybe the previous owners would welcome their animals back. At no cost, of course."

Jesse whipped off his Stetson, gazed skyward and

laughed as he wiped the back of his roughhewn hand across his forehead.

"How generous of you. But it would be next to impossible." His callousness faded as he continued. "They were killed in a car accident six months ago."

"Oh, I'm sorry. I didn't know."

It seemed Jonathan had neglected to tell her a lot of things about the ranch. Not that she'd asked him many questions. One look at the photos and she'd wanted to move as soon as possible. Now Miranda was desperate to get some clarification from her friend.

"They didn't have any children, so the house went to Fran's sister. Since she had no use for it, it went up for sale." Jesse pulled his hat down low, shielding his eyes. "You and I both bid on it. I lost and you won the whole shootin' match. I was only watching the place until the estate was settled."

Miranda supported herself against the truck. A house was one thing, but animals? She had plans of starting a small business in town once she moved to Ramble-wood. Only her ideas were more along the lines of a clothing boutique. This wasn't what she expected at all.

From what she could see of his face, he was distraught over the loss of his friends and home. Miranda felt a small pang of guilt. While she wanted a place to call home and to start a family of her own, she didn't want to destroy someone else's life in order to get it.

She'd soften her tone with him and try to get on friendlier terms. "So what exactly does a ranch manager do?" If she was lucky, maybe she could even convince him to stay and help her for a few days, or until she figured out what was going on here.

"I oversaw the entire spread, as well as being the head trainer."

"Trainer?" Miranda repeated.

"I train cutting horses."

Miranda stared blankly at Jesse.

He rolled his eyes. "Cutting horses are used to move cattle around, among other things."

"I see." A scene from an old Western flashed through Miranda's head. "I didn't realize people still did that."

"Sure they do." He took a deep breath. "Listen, I have another job waiting for me in Abilene, but I'll stay around for a bit and feed the livestock. I don't work for free, and I'm not staying long. Just long enough for you to decide what to do with all of this."

Bingo!

"Really? You'll stay?" Miranda saw a slight glimmer of hope. "That would be great!"

"Don't get ahead of yourself, I'm only here temporarily. What's your name?"

"Miranda. Miranda Archer," she said, eagerly holding out her hand.

He took her hand in his and turned her palm over once again. "It's not too bad. The sting will go away in a few minutes."

The gentleness of his touch sent her mind in the opposite direction of pain. *Maybe I can find out if cowboys really do roll in the hay.* Heat rose in her cheeks at the thought.

"Well, Miranda. Come on." Jesse motioned to her. "We've got plenty of work to do."

"Work?" Miranda glanced at the pile of her belongings packed into the truck. "I just got here. I haven't even had a chance to see inside my house."

She didn't wait for a response. Miranda retrieved a few bags and headed up the porch stairs. Jesse bounded ahead of her.

"Not now." He took the bags from her and dropped them on the porch. "Until you hire a new foreman you need to learn how to take care of these animals. Like I said, I'm not staying long."

He *couldn't* leave! What would she do?

"Show me around later." Miranda shooed him away.

She really was desperate to see the house and wasn't about to wait a minute longer. The house had played a major part in her move to Ramblewood: From the listing information the Realtor had emailed her, it had a great deal of charm and a homey quality. Ever since, Miranda pictured herself there, with a husband and a houseful of children. The fact it was a thousand miles away from Washington, D.C., was an added bonus.

"Let's get a few things straight, Miranda. I'm not your personal tour guide." Jesse took her arm and steered her down the stairs. "You can see the house on your own time. The sooner I show you what to do around here, the sooner I can be on my way."

He walked ahead to the stable entrance and waited for her. Miranda was torn. It was probably wise to pacify the cowboy for the time being. After buying the house and the truck, she only had enough money left to tide her over for a year. She not only needed help with the ranch, she needed a friend in town. Not an enemy.

"Oh, well, I'm sure this won't take long."

Inside, the pungent smell of hay assaulted her senses, causing her to sneeze. Jesse took a pair of leather gloves from his back pocket and gave them to her. He grabbed another pair from a shelf and put them on as he walked to the last stall.

"Do you have sneakers or work boots to put on?" he asked. "What am I asking? You wouldn't even know what *work boots* look like."

Miranda narrowed her eyes at him. "What's wrong with these?" She stuck out one foot, proud of her new red-and-turquoise leather cowboy boots. They sure were pretty.

"They haven't even been broken in yet. Those are meant for riding, not walking. You'll regret wearing them in five minutes flat."

"I'll be fine, thank you." She pushed a few long strands of hair behind her ears as she strutted past him.

"Suit yourself." Jesse unlatched the stall door and stepped in to stand beside a large gray horse. "Tell me. Do all rich city girls buy property without seeing it?"

Again with the insults?

"You don't quit do you?" Miranda tried to think of the shortest way to explain her situation. "My best friend is from San Antonio and he thought the Hill Country would be a perfect place for me to start over."

"What was so horrible you had to run away? I know! You ran out of places to shop."

Miranda chastised herself. This was her one shot at a new beginning. The citizens of Ramblewood didn't need to know what her life had been like before she arrived.

When she didn't respond, Jesse laughed as he adjusted a harness over the horse's head. He led the horse down the long corridor and outside, double-checking to make sure Miranda followed.

"Never walk close to the back end of a horse," Jesse said over his shoulder. "It's a surefire way to get kicked."

Miranda quickened her steps to put the equine's business end behind her.

"Surely I wasn't the only one who could have outbid you. Why take this out on me?"

Jesse ignored her and turned the horse loose in the corral with the others. Miranda rested her arms on the top rail of the fence while he returned to the stables. Fresh, clean air filled her lungs. She couldn't believe she was here, in Texas. On her land.

He reappeared with another horse. She fumbled with the latch as she tried to open the gate for him. With the flick of his thumb, Jesse swung it open, grinning at her.

Miranda closed the gate with Jesse still in the corral. He eyed her warily, stepped up on a fence rail and hopped over it, landing less than a foot in front of her. For a moment, Miranda thought he'd end up on top of her.

"You were the only other bidder," he said as he headed inside.

Why would that be? If he didn't want to expand on that information, she'd drag it out of him.

"There was no guarantee no one else would bid." Miranda was on his heels when he turned to face her.

"Everyone in Ramblewood knew I wanted this place," he snapped. "You don't get it, do you? They all knew this was my ranch."

Miranda held her ground. His intimidation tactics were not going to scare her this time.

"How was I supposed to know? And it's not your ranch. It's mine."

"I deserved Double Trouble!" he shouted.

"And you're about to get it if you shout at me one more time!"

Jesse flinched at her retort. This wasn't quite how she imagined her first day in Texas. She figured she'd see her house, walk around the property, maybe drive into town and have a bite to eat. Anything but this.

"Some welcoming committee you are," Miranda huffed.

"Sugar, if you're looking for a warm welcome, you're barking up the wrong tree."

"To think, I drove all the way here for this. I'm starting to regret it."

"Oh, goody." Jesse clasped his hands together in mock glee. "Does that mean you'll leave?"

"Not on your life." Miranda didn't appreciate his sarcasm. This was her home now. She wasn't about to let some cowboy chase her away.

As she opened her mouth to tell him where he could go, a horse neighed from inside the stables. Her mouth snapped shut.

What was she thinking? She couldn't send him away. He was the only one who could help her now. At least until Jonathan cleared up this mess.

From where she stood, the ranch seemed endless. It was a magnificent piece of land—the photographs hadn't done it justice. There was a small cottage behind the house, nestled amongst dogwoods. From beyond the white pasture fencing, fields of wildflowers faded into a copse of trees. A couple of bungalows stood alongside a dirt road that ran through the pastures, toward the hills. The ranch seemed to roll with the landscape. She understood why Jesse was so protective of someone turning it into a housing development. The Hill Country was all she dreamed of and more.

Jesse stood beside her as he took in the same view. When Miranda turned to face him she noticed his features darkened by sadness. She found herself stumbling for words to comfort him in some small way.

"It really is beautiful here," she said.

The wall between them needed to come down so they could work together. Miranda thought their mutual admiration for the land was a good start.

"Yes, it is. As long as you don't ruin it."

So much for that idea.

"Once again, I'm not going to ruin it. Give me a break, will you? I came here for some peace of mind."

"Peace of mind? What's been stressing you out, sugar?" Jesse eyed her top to bottom. "Your shopping sprees? Bet you're still using Daddy's credit cards to buy everything. You wouldn't know the meaning of an honest day's work if it bit you on the—"

"I beg your pardon?"

"Don't beg, sugar. It doesn't become you. Now come on, we have work to do."

Miranda went with him, willingly this time, toward the stables. He removed a wheelbarrow and shovel from a storage room and pushed it toward her.

"Start with the first stall and work your way around. Shovel it completely out, down to the floor. Old bedding goes in the large green container out back for composting. We use the last stall on the left to store fresh bedding. Open five bags in the stall and spread it around till you have about a two-inch depth. I'll check in on you later and show you how to wet the bedding to fluff it up. Good luck. You'll need it."

JESSE KEPT HIS LAUGHTER in check until he'd turned the last horse out in the corral. He'd never seen a woman so rip-roaring mad in all his life. After her hissy fit, she'd settled down and got to work mucking the stalls. She had to learn the ropes somehow.

He had to admit, even with all the aggravation she caused him, he sure did enjoy the sway of her hips when she walked and the way her hair fell free, to the middle of her back. She was a looker. There was no doubt about it.

Jesse knew the instant Miranda climbed from her truck, the name Double Trouble finally rung true. She was shapelier than a Coke bottle and had green eyes the color of spring leaves. A woman like her could only make a man's life difficult. And she'd proven to be no exception so far.

Not only had he lost everything, he'd lost it to a beautiful blonde. But there was something different about her. She possessed such a deep self-confidence yet her face reflected a loneliness that reminded him of a child on the first day of a new school.

When Fran Carter's sister put the ranch up for sale, Jesse was livid. He'd offered Caroline more than a fair price for the place. Nevertheless, she had been determined to get all she could for it.

It didn't matter one iota that Fran and Ed Carter had spoken at great length about their intentions to sell Double Trouble to Jesse. They treated him like a son and Jesse considered himself blessed to have a second family. While the Carters enjoyed the ranch, the house had needed more and more repairs. They were tired and wanted a stress-free retirement in a smaller house near town. Then tragedy had struck.

Though Caroline had been devastated by her sister's and brother-in-law's deaths, when it came to the ranch all Caroline could see were dollar signs. From her Seattle home, she'd arranged the sale of the antiques and most of the furniture only two days after Fran's funeral. Assuming the ranch would run itself she didn't realize half of what Jesse brought in training horses was his to keep. Combined with the vet and feed bills, Double Trouble cut into her bottom line. Thanks to Jesse spreading the word around town not to buy the horses and cattle, she gave up and left them to the new owner.

After Jesse had forgone his father's offer to work on his family's ranch when he graduated high school, the Carters had hired him. Despite the fact he loved his family and respected his brothers' decisions to work there, he didn't want anything handed to him.

Bridle Dance was his great-grandfather's legacy. And while he was proud of his family, Jesse wanted a legacy of his own. Now fifteen years later, he had to walk away from what he believed would have been his.

Just when he thought his time on Double Trouble was over, he had to contend with Miranda. The sight of her stepping out of that new truck made his blood boil. The woman didn't know one end of a bull from the other. Now she owned his ranch. The last thing he wanted was to witness the destruction of the place he loved.

Common decency told him to show her enough to get by. Help her hire a foreman and then be on his way. Another part told him to stay in case she floundered and decided to hotfoot it back home.

If her expensive jeans and new boots were any indication, there was no way she could handle running a ranch. If his instincts were right, maybe Double Trouble would be his after all.

A girl like her wasn't used to this type of life but she was about to learn the gritty details. And maybe, just maybe, she would realize this was not for her.

A few hours later, Jesse checked in on Miranda. He expected to see one, maybe two stalls mucked. Instead, he was amazed to see every stall clean and freshly bedded.

He gave her credit. It couldn't have been easy for her, but she accomplished it anyway. Jesse had to admire her tenacity.

Jesse found Miranda behind the stables, rubbing her feet through the leather of her boots. His dog, Max, who was apparently *not* man's best friend, was wagging his tail as he sat beside her. *Traitor.* He hurried inside before she saw him. He whistled a Western tune to warn her he was around the corner.

"Here you are," Jesse said as Miranda wobbled to her feet. "I see you met Max. For the record, he doesn't come with the ranch."

"It's all finished." Wisps of hair fell from her make-shift ponytail. Dust and sweat covered her chest and arms. She looked as though she was ready to drop. On the other hand, maybe it was the guaranteed blisters on her feet that were making her face scrunch up as it did. "Now, if you don't mind, I'm going to see my house."

Jesse let her get halfway to the porch before he called to her.

"You best be careful where you wander off to." Jesse warned. "You never know who or what might be prowling around here."

Miranda spun around, her eyes wide.

"Don't look so surprised." Jesse feigned concern. "This is Texas, after all. We have snakes and all sorts of wild animals around these parts. Never mind what the livestock will do if provoked."

Miranda eyed him warily as he walked toward her.

"Remember the old saying," he whispered in her hair as he brushed past her. "You mess with the bull, and you're going to get horned."

The corner of her mouth rose in a sly smile.

"Be careful, cowboy," she said as she continued to her house. "You just may be the one to get horned."

Jesse caught her elbow before she could go inside.

"Listen, little girl." He encircled her waist and drew her close. "Watch it before you get yourself in a whole heap of trouble."

Miranda didn't break her gaze, she matched it. Tiny droplets formed above her lip. He'd gamble those lips tasted salty right about now. Before he lost complete control, Jesse stepped aside.

She attempted a smile, but fatigue won out. Jesse hadn't considered how long she had driven to get here. From the looks of her, all night. He felt like a heel. He bossed her around for half the day and didn't even allow her to see her house.

"Are there any more chores or may I be excused?" Miranda stood with a look of defiance he had never seen before.

Except maybe in a mirror.

"Go in and see your new house." Jesse kicked at some hay. "Get yourself settled and grab something to eat. I'll finish up out here."

Miranda didn't protest. She limped past him, toward the porch.

The urge was too great for him to resist. "I told you those new boots were going to be a killer."

Miranda stopped. He half expected her to give him another tongue-lashing. Instead, she hesitated briefly then continued on walking.

It was time to get back to work while he still had duties here at the ranch. "She's something else," he said to General Lee as Jesse led him out of the corral.

The horse nodded his head as if he understood. Jesse watched Miranda hobble up the porch stairs. Each step was a well-calculated movement.

"I almost feel sorry for her." Jesse latched the stall door once the horse was inside. "It must be rough. A new town, a new home and a jackass who pushes her around."

General Lee's muzzle smacked Jesse's head into one of the stall posts.

"Watch it!" Jesse rubbed the side of his head. "What's gotten into you today? If you're trying to knock some sense into me, you can forget it. She's trouble with a capital *T* and I don't give a damn what happens to her."

The gelding turned in his stall and presented Jesse with a rear view.

"Thanks, pal." He stormed off to the stable office. He knew he needed to apologize to Miranda for the way he'd treated her. More important, he needed to find a way to convince her to sell him the ranch. If he played his cards right, he could do it all with the help of one person and nobody would be the wiser.

Jesse picked up the phone and dialed.

Chapter Two

Miranda sat in the kitchen, soaking her feet in a small aluminum tub she found in the pantry. They were covered in blisters and ached more than they ever had in her life.

Note to self: wear sneakers next time. Score one for the cowboy.

She never thought she would make it through the first stall, let alone the last one. But she'd be damned if she'd let a man get the best of her. Who did he think he was, anyway?

If he tells me what to do one more time, I'll...well, I'll do something. That's for sure. The phrase "where the sun don't shine" came to mind.

She tried twice to reach Jonathan, only to get his voice mail. He talked to her on the phone most of the previous night to keep her company during her drive. She couldn't imagine why he wasn't answering.

Until she figured out what to do, she needed to bite her tongue when it came to Jesse. But it didn't mean she'd allow him to boss her around and make fun of her. Yes, she needed some lessons on ranch life. Yes, he was the perfect one to show her the ropes. But mucking the stalls? That was a man's job. She could feed the horses or put out fresh water or whatever the heck people did on a ranch full of animals.

When Jonathan first mentioned Double Trouble she knew in her heart it was where she belonged. Even before she saw the photographs. If anyone knew the kind of life she desired, it was Jonathan. Not only was he her best friend, he was the brother she never had. He was the only one she trusted with her hopes and dreams. Now here she was, unable to reach him and away from everyone she knew. She was officially a ranch owner. A ranch owner with horses and cattle.

Don't forget the chickens.

Although it was an extraordinary and rare event, winning the lottery hadn't quite been the highlight of Miranda's year. After what she had been through, it came more as a relief. While it wasn't enough money to guarantee she'd never have to work again, it was enough to buy Double Trouble and her truck outright. A sheet of paper with her finances lay before her. Every dime was carefully budgeted. And if she played her cards right, she had a year of padding built in.

Miranda shivered. She wasn't sure if she was cold and scared or overwhelmed by the vastness of the ranch. Choosing the latter as a reasonable explanation, Miranda decided to unpack the items she'd brought with her. Then maybe the old place would feel more like home. Starting with a pair of flip-flops. She knew they were in one of these boxes.

Furniture shopping was on the top of her list for tomorrow. She didn't have much left after she'd donated almost everything she owned to Goodwill before she left D.C.

Miranda noted every nook and cranny of the house.

There were very few furnishings left behind. Much less than she had figured. A large drop leaf farm table and chairs, some bookcases and a few end tables were all that remained. Considering the sale included the contents of the ranch, she expected more furniture, and fewer animals. It was only day one and she already had to adjust her budget.

After choosing which room would be her bedroom, Miranda went downstairs by way of a narrow staircase that led to the kitchen. The old door creaked as she opened it, causing her to smile. Most people would lubricate the old iron hinges. She rather liked the homey sound.

Years of smoke darkened the bricks above the fireplace and bread oven. Another bit of charm she would preserve.

This is where I'm meant to be.

She could almost hear the love and laughter that used to fill these empty rooms. When she closed her eyes, she saw her own dreams of yesteryear play out before her. She opened them and envisioned children running in from outside, muddy feet leaving footprints behind them on the worn floor. Memories of her past faded. It was time for new ones.

By the time Miranda unloaded her truck and rental trailer, it was midafternoon. Taking a bottle of pink lemonade and a peanut butter and jelly sandwich from her cooler, she surveyed the ranch through the screen door.

Miranda had to face the fact that Jonathan knew about Jesse and the livestock. Why else would he be dodging her calls? His secretary claimed he was away on business for the remainder of the week, but he'd mentioned nothing about that yesterday. How convenient.

When she tried his cell phone, all she heard was Jonathan's chipper voice mail greeting. After the last message Miranda left, she'd be amazed if he ever spoke to her again. Why didn't he clue her in on everything before she arrived? She'd had enough surprises over the past year to last a lifetime.

"How am I ever going to manage this place?"

"With a little help and a lot of kindness."

Miranda jumped at the response. A middle-aged woman, with skin the color of cinnamon, poked her head through the door.

"I didn't mean to startle you, dear," the woman said as she let herself in. She carried an armful of brown paper sacks filled to the hilt with cleaning products. She placed them on the table, then beelined for the boxes Miranda had left on the counter.

"Excuse me." Miranda tried to get the woman's attention. "Excuse me, um, whoever you are."

"The name's Mable Promise," she said as she glanced around the room. "Jesse reckoned you might need a helping hand, or two, around here. We sure do have our work cut out for us. This house sat empty for way too long. Needs a good going-over, if I do say so myself."

"I don't understand." Jesse told the woman she needed help? "I—"

"There's nothing to understand. Now come on. We have plenty to do by the looks of things." Mable directed Miranda to a stack of unopened boxes while she worked her way through the pots and pans. "Well, don't just stand there stewin' in your own juices. If we're going to make this ranch work, we best get started."

Miranda struggled to speak, choosing to chew on

her bottom lip instead. Who was this woman unpacking her utensils?

"I'll wash everything here. Do you have fresh linens on the beds?"

"Beds? I don't have any beds. I don't have any furniture really. I'm planning to go shopping tomorrow. Tonight I'll camp out on the living room floor."

"Well, we can't have that!" Mable dried her hands and walked over to the screen door. "Jesse! Get on in here!"

The apples of Mable's cheeks glowed as she smiled at Miranda. She had welcoming eyes. Caring and compassionate, like the eyes a mother has for her child. Miranda could only guess what it would have felt like if her own mother had once looked at her that way.

Jesse stood in the doorway. A perfect silhouette of his body stood in contrast to the afternoon sun. Miranda's pulse began to quicken.

"Drive Miranda into town and pick up a mattress and box spring. I don't want her sleeping on the hard floor. Lord knows it needs a good scrubbing. If you hurry, you can get to Mayfield's before they close."

Mable bustled about the kitchen as she spoke, her feet moving as fast as her tongue. Jesse laughed. This was apparently normal to him. He seemed at home and relaxed as he watched the robust woman. Until the woman stopped in her tracks and glared at him.

"Uh-oh." Jesse groaned then scrambled for the door. "Now go on…git!"

Mable chased them outside and down the porch stairs with a dish towel. Miranda yelped as they crossed the yard to her truck. She'd forgotten she was barefoot. Her blisters sure hadn't.

Her shoes were inside. She imagined the wrath she would incur if she went back in and asked for them. A few seconds later, the screen door swung wide and Mable tossed a pair of flip-flops down the stairs. Carefully, she slid her feet into them. As much as they hurt, she wasn't about to let Jesse see her pain.

"You didn't have to do this." Miranda nodded toward the kitchen. "I don't know what to say."

"Forget it. It was my way of apologizing for the way I treated you earlier."

Miranda wasn't quite sure if she should thank him or strangle him. A stranger just chased her out of her home and took over her kitchen.

"Who is she, anyway?"

"Mable's been a family friend for as long as I can recall." Jesse leaned on the truck fender. "She worked for the Carters before the accident. Lived in that cottage over there. Figured she could work here again since you're going to need all the help you can get."

"Work for me? Look, I don't know how much money you think I have, but—"

"As long as she can live on Double Trouble, she'll be happy with whatever you can pay. Her husband passed on a few years ago. He ran the cattle end of the business before they downsized it. They shared their final years together here. This place has sentimental value to her."

Miranda sensed a guilt trip coming on. "I'm sorry to hear that but—"

"Word to the wise, sugar, don't ever let Mable hear you say you feel sorry for her. She'll tan your hide for sure."

"Oh, I didn't mean—"

"I know what you meant. It's Mable who won't."

Miranda felt all control over her ranch slip further away with each word out of her mouth.

"Nice rig. Must have set you back a bit," Jesse said, as he inspected the black quad cab pickup. "Not that it would matter much to you."

"What's that supposed to mean?"

"Nothing. Nothing at all." Jesse jumped in the driver's seat. "Toss me the keys."

"Thanks for the offer, but I can drive myself, without any help from you."

"You have no idea where you're going," Jesse said. "The center of town is nowhere near the interstate, which I assume is the way you came in. You'll get lost on these back roads."

"If I can manage to get here all the way from D.C., I think I can handle a little trip into town. Just point me in the right direction."

"Suit yourself." Jesse pointed toward the main road. "It's that way."

An endless dirt road lay before the ranch. The same dirt road she drove down when she arrived. And she didn't recall seeing any signs for a town ahead along the way.

"Sure you don't want me to tag along? I can help you try out those beds." He winked, his intentions all too clear.

"Let me get this straight." Miranda smiled. "You don't even like me, yet you're offering to sleep with me?"

"Honey, I don't have to like you in order to bed you for the night."

Miranda ignored his comment as she climbed in the truck. She headed down the dusty road, in the opposite direction she had come earlier. She had grown accustomed to her new truck over the past few days. Anything beat the broken-down cracker box she'd driven for the past six years.

After she passed three unmarked turnoffs, she decided to try her luck on the next one. It was next to impossible to tell which led to ranches and which ones were legitimate roads. Acres upon acres of pastures and crops lined the narrow lane, but there was no sign of a town.

A few attempts down others brought her to an intersection identical to the one she'd passed a few miles before. Now she was lost.

An hour later, she found herself in front of Double Trouble—no closer to town than she was before she left.

"Shoot!"

Miranda drove down the ranch drive, watching for signs of Jesse. The noise her tires made on top of the cattle guards made an unnoticed entrance highly unlikely. There was no way she was about to admit she'd never made it to town. He would enjoy it a little too much. She parked the truck and ran up the stairs. Mable would give her directions and she would try again tomorrow.

Miranda threw open the screen door and smacked face-first into Jesse's chest.

"How was town, sugar?" He raised a brow as if to challenge her.

"I...uh." Miranda tried to sidestep the cowboy, but he braced his arms on either side of the doorjamb.

"What was it you were saying?"

Jesse's wicked grin said it all. He knew.

"So what?" Miranda pushed him aside and stormed into the kitchen. "So, I never made it into town."

"What? I didn't hear you."

"I said I never made it to town!" Miranda shouted. "Are you deaf or just stupid?"

Miranda swore she felt steam rise from her skin. In a matter of hours, Jesse learned the right buttons to push. In one day, he managed to infuriate her more than most men did in a lifetime.

"My hearing's fine, but you appear to be the stupid one," he said as he strolled out the door. "Couldn't even get your sorry self to town. Guess you'll be sleeping on the floor tonight after all."

The screen door slammed in his wake.

"Oh!" Miranda stomped her feet.

"We'll have none of that, dear." Mable joined Miranda as they watched Jesse's retreat to the foreman's house. "Pay no mind to him. His feathers are still ruffled over this place."

"None of which was my fault," Miranda added. "What's his problem, anyway? He's so angry and bitter."

"Pride. Pure pride." Grabbing a bottle of pink lemonade out of Miranda's cooler, Mable opened it and took a sip. "Eww. I need to teach you how to make this stuff from scratch. It sure would taste better."

Miranda felt her anger leaving her as she stared at the old kitchen floor. A layer of wax left a thick residue on the stained linoleum. She eyed a box of steel wool Mable had brought and got up to fill a bucket of water. On her hands and knees, Miranda began to scrub. Mable followed suit, and the two of them slowly began stripping the floor. It was cathartic in its own way.

"He's a tough one to figure out," Mable said.

Miranda only nodded in agreement.

"Jesse's father never forgave him when he opted out of the family business." Mable continued to scour as she spoke. "It's not so much he didn't want to be a part of the family ranch. He wanted to build one of his own."

"And that didn't go over well with Jesse's dad?"

"Langtry men are all stubborn. The whole lot of them. Jesse despises having anything handed to him." She plunged the steel wool into the water. "If he had joined his brothers and taken over Bridle Dance, he wouldn't think that was much of an accomplishment."

"But it's different. It's an inheritance."

Miranda would have given her eyeteeth to have a family. Let alone one who wanted her to join the family business.

"I know it. But Jesse never saw things that way. And his father never saw it Jesse's way. Don't get me wrong. Jesse respects his brothers for their decisions, but it wasn't what he wanted out of life."

"Sounds like he has something to prove."

Miranda understood how he felt in that regard. A year of *should haves* and *what ifs* had passed since her mother's death, combined with a broken engagement, and she still felt that way.

"He does. To himself. Jesse wasn't in the rodeo spotlight like his three brothers always were. He's an honest man. Just wants to make a life for himself. One he can be proud of."

"I guess it's noble when you think about it."

While it wasn't a choice Miranda would have made, she understood his reasons, to a certain degree. She always dreamed of what life would be like if she had been part of a large family instead of the disaster she came from. Jesse, on the other hand, felt the need to break free from his.

The grass is always greener.

"Jesse demands things his way. His way was buying this ranch. Years ago, the Carters promised to sell it to him when they retired. He saved every penny he ever made to buy this place. He was downright devastated when he lost it."

"I'm sorry, Mable, but I refuse to feel bad about buying this place."

"I'm not asking you to." Mable stood and rubbed the small of her back. "I'm just making you aware of why he's acting the way he is. In the end, he only wants a family of his own."

So the cowboy was human.

"Why doesn't he go back to Bridle Dance now?" Miranda wondered aloud. "At least for a little while, to regroup. Instead of this new job in Abilene."

"Heaven knows his father tried to talk him into it. Jesse even considered it, for a spell. But like I said, he's a stubborn one. I'm surprised he's agreed to stay on and help you out."

"He's staying on for the sake of the animals," Miranda said. "Not me."

"Maybe so. But he's still here."

"For the time being." A deep voice echoed throughout the kitchen.

Startled, Miranda knocked the bucket of water, sloshing half of it onto the floor. She scrambled for a roll of paper towels while avoiding any eye contact with him. She now had more of an appreciation for the man who stood before her. However, she wasn't about to let her guard down around him just yet.

"Instead of eavesdropping," Mable chided, "go see if you can find a mop."

Without a word, Jesse left the kitchen.

Annoyed at the ease with which Jesse unsettled her, Miranda attempted to soak up the black water. This was crazy. *Why does this man have such a hold over me?* Whenever he was around, she was as nervous as a schoolgirl.

"Well, no sense crying over spilt milk," Mable said, getting to her feet. "We best head into town and pick up some food." Mable wiped her hands on a dish towel. "I'm famished."

"Don't let her drive," Jesse interjected. He was standing there holding a rope mop like a knight ready to joust. "She'll take you round in a circle and back again. You'll end up starving to death."

"We'll have none of that," Mable chastised him, pushing Miranda out the door. "Make yourself useful, Jesse. Mop up the floor."

The woman ignored Jesse's grumblings while Miranda found it impossible not to smile. Mable sure could put Jesse in his place at the drop of a dime.

"I'll show you where everything is in town," Mable said as she turned the key in the ignition of the old car. A loud backfire almost knocked Miranda out of her seat. "Then tomorrow you can buy yourself something decent to sleep on."

"Thank you."

Miranda hated to admit it, but she was grateful to Jesse for staying around and bringing Mable to the ranch to help her. Maybe he wasn't so heartless after all.

"Mable, I need to talk to you about salary and what I owe you for the supplies you bought."

"Not now, child. There will be time enough for money talk later on."

"But—"

"I'm staying with my sister until I move back to the ranch," Mable interrupted. "Why don't you bunk with us tonight?"

"Thank you for the offer," Miranda said. "But I really want to sleep in my own house. About the money—"

"First house?"

Miranda shook her head and smiled. She could take a hint. She made a mental note to discuss Mable's salary in the morning.

"Yes. Something I've wanted for a long time. Only I never could afford it."

"Come into some money recently?"

"Accidentally, yes." Miranda stared out the window. Mable didn't press further and Miranda didn't offer. Some things were better left unsaid. At least for the time being.

Chapter Three

The cool morning air greeted Jesse as he stepped out-side. A few more weeks would bring the onslaught of summer. The Hill Country's steady breeze was a bless-ing throughout the warmer months, keeping the heat at a tolerable level. Still, Jesse liked to complete any form of hard labor before the noonday sun.

Outside the foreman's house, a panting tongue and a wagging tail greeted him and Jesse bent to scratch the dog behind the ears. Max had been his ranch hand for the past five years, essential in training the cutting horses for roundup. His four-legged pal was the only thing around here these days that didn't cause him any aggravation.

Speaking of aggravation.

Jesse glanced toward the main house. Mable wouldn't arrive for a few more hours. That meant he could spend some time with Miranda, showing her, firsthand, how hard ranch life truly was.

Dinner the night before went well enough. Mable's fried chicken, mashed potatoes and buttermilk gravy were delicious enough to make his toes curl. A home-cooked meal was one of the many things he missed after the Carters had died. Every now and then, Mable

would stop by the ranch with a plate of food or his fa-
vorite, spicy chocolate-mince pie. She always thought
about everyone else.

Miranda didn't seem to know what to make of the
fried chicken at first. She picked at it, and then tasted
a small piece. After that, there was no going back. She
dove right in and devoured the golden breast. Even lick-
ing her fingers clean.

Didn't they serve real food in D.C.?

She disappeared a few times to try to call someone
from her cell phone. When her frustration got the best of
her, she joined them on the front porch. The remainder
of the evening, she devoted her full attention to Mable.
Of course, she paid no mind to him whatsoever. It was
as if he weren't even there.

Mable recounted the ranch's history and told stories about some of Ramblewood's quirkier residents.
Like the time Karen Johnson woke to Charlie Slater's
prize mule braying in her bedroom window after it escaped its corral. Or when the old timers broke into the
Ramblewood jail in the middle of the night and locked
themselves in cells, with their horses, protesting the
No Horses on Main Street law. The law was quickly
reversed.

While Miranda was leery of some things, she
laughed until she cried at others. Jesse wasn't sure if
she believed half of what she heard. Nonetheless, she
seemed to enjoy herself.

Miranda did need a lesson or two about the ways of
the residents in these parts. Mable informed him she
was none too friendly toward the townsfolk at the grocery store. He could only assume the people in D.C.

were not a welcoming lot, judging by her amazement at Mable alone. This, too, could work to his advantage.

"Might as well wake up Little Miss Ray of Sunshine." Max barked in agreement and ran up the porch stairs. Dawn was on the horizon and there were chores to do.

Jesse bounded up the stairs and tried the knob. Locked. He peered through the window and made out a motionless sleeping bag. He could have given her one of the mattresses from the bunkhouse like Mable asked him to before she left. But it would have made things too easy on her. Heck, he already did her a favor by hiring Mable.

You did yourself that favor, pal.

He knocked on the door. Nothing.

"Miranda!" he hollered. The sleeping bag stirred and then went still again. "Miranda!"

Miranda shot upright and scanned the room. After she spotted Jesse, he saw she was none too thrilled to have him as her first vision of the day.

She struggled with the zipper on the sleeping bag. Unable to open it, she hopped to her feet and slid the bag down around her ankles. When she attempted to step out of it, she tripped and fell to the floor.

Jesse held his laughter as he watched Miranda kick the bag. She leaped to her feet and tried to gain what composure she had left. She limped to the door and opened it.

"What time is it?" Miranda peered out on the porch. "It's not even light out."

She wore yellow flannel boxer shorts and a white cotton T-shirt. Her hair was wild and skin free of any makeup. Her legs seemed endless and her shirt accentuated the rise and fall of her breasts.

Miranda followed his gazed and folded her arms across her chest, feigning a shiver.

Beautiful or not, if he was ever going to get her off the ranch he needed to work her to death. Once she had a good dose of daily life on Double Trouble, she would pack up and head home in no time.

"Rise and shine, sugar." Jesse took off his hat as he entered the kitchen. "We've got a big day ahead of us."

The kitchen was spotless. Miranda had completely stripped the wax from the floor and reapplied a fresh coat. A coffeemaker and freestanding electric mixer replaced the boxes on the counter. She must have gone back to work when he and Mable left for the night.

"Get dressed and we'll head out."

Miranda faced him, bewildered. She shook her head, turned and went into the living room. For a moment, he thought she was about to lie down and go back to sleep. Instead, she grabbed a duffel bag from the floor, dragged some clothes out of it and headed to the bathroom without so much as a word.

A few moments later, she emerged, freshly scrubbed and her hair tied up in a ponytail. When she put on a pair of old sneakers, Jesse tried to hide his amusement.

"Yes, I know. I should have listened to you and worn different shoes yesterday. You don't have to rub it in."

"I didn't say a word." Jesse grinned.

"Your look says it all." Miranda stood and smoothed her hands over her jeans. "What's on the agenda for today?"

"First, we need to turn the horses out," Jesse said as he led her through the door. Max greeted her with a playful bark. "Then we need to do some maintenance on one of the stalls."

"Turn the horses out?" Miranda questioned over her shoulder, almost missing the first porch step.

"Watch it." Jesse caught her arm before she fell. "You certainly aren't the most graceful of creatures are you?"

"What do you mean 'turn the horses out'?" she repeated, ignoring his insult.

"I mean putting them in the pasture over there so they can graze and exercise. Grazing prevents colic. It's something I need to teach you to watch for."

"I thought only babies got colic."

"Sugar, you have a lot to learn." Jesse laughed.

Priceless was the only way to describe her puzzled expression. Jesse placed his hand on the small of her back as he escorted her across the yard. The simple act shot heat through him like a lightning bolt.

Sure, he had touched plenty of women in much more intimate places. They just never affected him this way. Not only was it a feeling he wasn't used to, it was one he never expected. Especially with the woman who stole his ranch.

This is going to be a long day.

Since his bossiness didn't yield the results he'd expected yesterday, he decided to take a gentler approach today, similar to the one he used when training horses. He'd break her in slowly, offering a reward here and there.

"Tell you what. Let's get the horses situated and then head into town for some breakfast."

He might as well take her to Mayfield's to buy a bed while he was at it. *I wouldn't mind taking one for a little test drive, either.* Miranda didn't take too kindly to the suggestion yesterday. After waking her up at the crack of dawn, he didn't think she would take too kindly to it now. It didn't stop him from envisioning himself waking up beside her.

What the heck has come over me?

To clear his mind, Jesse taught Miranda how to halter a horse. With General Lee as his guinea pig, he demonstrated the right and wrong way to approach a horse. Once he felt she understood, he let her practice.

After she faltered a few times, he stood behind her, guiding her arms with his. The softness of her hands combined with the vanilla scent of her hair almost sent him into a tailspin. This was supposed to clear his mind?

What was I thinking?

After a few attempts, Miranda got the hang of it. Still visibly intimidated by the horse's size, she led him from his stall. Once she led her third horse to pasture, her shoulders were back and a hint of a smile began to appear.

"That was so incredible!" Miranda said as she closed the corral gate for the last horse. "They follow me wherever I lead them."

"You wait," Jesse warned. "It's not all fun and games around here. This was the easiest part of your day. Come on. Let's get some breakfast."

Miranda tossed Jesse the keys to her truck.

"Oh, you must be daffy if you're allowing me to drive your precious chariot."

Miranda stuck her tongue out as she got in the passenger seat. As childish as it was, Jesse found the gesture charming. Under other circumstances, he would have asked her out on a date. She was determined and so far, proved herself a hard worker. All qualities he wanted in a woman. One little flaw got in his way. She stole his ranch.

As he drove into town, she pulled a notepad out of the center console. He couldn't believe it. Miranda was taking notes, counting streets and houses. She was obviously determined not to get herself lost the next time she ventured out on her own.

"Stop here!" Miranda shrieked, almost causing Jesse to drive off the road.

Before the truck came to a complete stop, Miranda had the door open. She jumped down and sprinted toward the furniture at a yard sale on the side of the road.

"I love it!" Miranda cried as she ran her hand over the old dresser. "How much?"

No please! No furniture! You're not staying long enough to warrant furniture. You only need a bed.

Miranda's purchases at the yard sale included a dresser, an iron bed frame, a sideboard, a few rocking chairs and a buffet.

"We have to return for the buffet and the chairs," Jesse groaned. "There's no more room in the truck."

Jesse inwardly fumed. There was plenty to do at the ranch and they had already killed a good portion of the morning. The last thing he wanted to do today was move a bunch of furniture around. He would have figured her the type who wanted new things, not pieces in dire need of refinishing. Frustration began to set in. He wanted her out of Ramblewood and fast. Yet here she was, nesting like a mother bird.

"It's all right, Jesse," Beau Bradley said. "Aaron and I will drop them by the ranch later on. It's good seeing someone in the old Carter place again."

"No comment." Jesse held his tongue to keep from

speaking his true feelings on the subject. "You sure you want to be saddled lugging this stuff over?"

"No trouble at all."

Jesse didn't want the old man to overexert himself. Which he had a tendency to do on most occasions.

"Thanks!" Miranda beamed.

"Anytime." Beau tipped his hat and waved goodbye.

Back on course, Jesse steered the truck onto the main road and headed toward town.

"Where are you going?" Miranda looked through the rear window at her purchases. "We need to unload the truck."

"After we eat and buy a bed."

"But someone will steal it!" Miranda's breath quickened.

"Steal what?" Jesse shot her a sidelong glance.

"My furniture!" She pointed out the window. "It's sitting there, in the open."

"Not around here they won't." Jesse laughed. "Listen, if you're going to live here, you best get yourself accustomed to our way of life. People here are friendly. They lend a hand to one another. No one even locks their doors at night. There's no need to worry about anyone stealing your furniture. What do you want with this stuff, anyway? It all needs to be refinished."

"I know. I can't wait to get started." Miranda looked gleeful at the prospect.

"You?" Jesse asked in disbelief. "What do you know about wood refinishing?"

"Plenty." Miranda jutted her chin in the air. "I read all about it in a magazine."

He laughed. Instead of arguing with him, she turned on the radio, drowning out any possibility of a conversation. From the corner of his eye, he watched Miranda mouth the words to the Tim McGraw song. The girl did her homework. He wondered if they even had country music in D.C.

Miranda hesitated when he stopped the truck in front of The Magpie. The redbrick luncheonette didn't look like an intimidating place to him with its white vinyl bird cutouts that decorated the large picture window. But something was causing her to hesitate. Then he realized she was still worried about her furniture.

"Give it a rest, Miranda." Jesse held the door open to the luncheonette. "No one will steal your precious furniture."

All eyes were on Miranda as she walked through the door. It was very obvious everyone had heard Jesse's comment. He was as embarrassed as she was right about now.

He led her to a booth, exchanging a few pleasantries along the way. The luncheonette was small. Four booths lined one wall, with a handful of tables close by. Originally a bakery, owner Maggie Dalton chose the name The Magpie after her husband had vetoed the name Maggie's Buns. Over the years, The Magpie grew into a place where some folks ate every meal. It was the spot to go to catch up on Ramblewood's latest gossip.

Or witness it, as the case may be today.

"Well, hello there, Jesse."

A stunning redhead winked as she set two cups of coffee and a creamer on the table. Her short pink uniform and white apron accentuated her slender figure. As many times as he'd asked Bridgett out, she'd always turned him down flat.

"Hey, Bridgett." Jesse turned sideways in the booth. "How's your mom doing?"

"Much better now. The cast's coming off this week. After some rehab, she'll be able to get around on her own."

"Must be a nuisance," Jesse continued, ignoring Miranda's glares. She could wait a moment longer and learn the meaning of the word *patience*.

"Don't I know it. For me as much as her. I have to work all day, then go home and take her every place she needs to go."

"Be sure to give her my best."

Miranda cleared her throat loudly until Jesse acknowledged her.

"Bridgett, this here is Miranda. She bought the old Carter place."

"It's a pleasure, Miranda." Bridgett smiled sweetly. "You need anything, you just holler, you hear?"

"Thanks." Miranda shrugged, dismissing Bridgett's sincerity.

Jesse shot her a warning glare. Bridgett shrugged and took a pencil from behind her ear.

"The usual for you, hon?"

"That'd be great," Jesse said.

"What will you have, dear?"

"Do you have anything low fat?" Miranda wrinkled up her nose as she perused the menu.

"She'll have pancakes and sausage." Jesse scowled, daring her to challenge him.

"You got it. They'll be out in a few." Bridgett winked at Jesse again as she walked toward the kitchen.

"I could have ordered for myself." Miranda grabbed

a napkin from the dispenser and wiped the table. "I'm on a diet."

"You look fine." Jesse snatched the napkin from her hands. "And you're going to need a big breakfast to get through today."

Miranda slumped backward in the booth. Every so often, someone would turn and stare at her.

"What are they all looking at?" Miranda said between clenched teeth.

"The person who stole my ranch. I told you. All of Ramblewood was behind me on this."

While Jesse appreciated the support he received from the townsfolk, he wasn't prepared for all the glaring and whispering he was seeing before him. Maybe coming here wasn't such a good idea after all.

"Well, they don't have to be so rude about it." Miranda's voice rose.

"Would you pipe down?" He reached for her hands across the top of the table.

"I will not pipe down!" she shouted. "Who do you think you are bossing me around every ten seconds? I'm really getting tired of it."

Embarrassed, Jesse squeezed Miranda's hands in his and tried to soothe her.

"I'm sorry. Please, calm down."

Jesse wanted nothing more than to leave the luncheonette. He had more than his fill of this mouthy northerner for one morning. Bringing her here was a mistake.

"Is it true you bought Double Trouble so you could turn it into a housing development?"

Jesse hung his head. This couldn't have come at a

worse time. Why had he ever told Charlotte Hargrove what he thought the new owner's plans were?

Because you know she has a big mouth and would tell the whole town.

Miranda slowly scanned the prim woman standing before her. Jesse held his breath sensing a major blow-out was about to take place.

"What did you ask me?" Miranda released herself from Jesse's grasp.

Miranda's words were slow and deliberate. Jesse watched the heat rise in her face and her pupils dilate. Ready to do battle.

"The way I hear it, you're turning Double Trouble into a housing development."

The entire room grew quiet. All eyes focused on Miranda.

"Look, I don't know who you are—"

"Charlotte," Jesse interrupted. "I don't think now is the time to discuss this."

"No! I want to hear what she has to say." Miranda eyed Jesse warily. "Tell me…Charlotte, is it? What else have you heard?"

"You're going to ruin a century's worth of history by tearing apart Double Trouble."

"Now, I wonder where you could have heard that from." Miranda slid out of the booth.

"Miranda, please sit down." Jesse tried to grab her hand but she snatched it away.

"May I have your attention please?" Miranda addressed the luncheonette. "As if I don't already."

Jesse crossed his arms in front of him on the table and lowered his head. His plan backfired. Breakfast was supposed to relax her. To prepare her for the day ahead.

He even wanted to learn a little more about her. It wasn't supposed to be a free-for-all in the middle of town.

"Not that my plans are any of your concern, but I would like to set the record straight."

Brace yourself. This is going to be a doozy.

Everyone in The Magpie hung on Miranda's every word.

"I didn't buy Double Trouble to build a housing development. I bought it to live on," Miranda said in a calm, steady voice. "And if any of you have a problem with that, deal with it!"

So much for calm.

Jesse glared at Miranda when she sat down. He couldn't believe what he had just witnessed. The entire town would catch wind of it in a half hour flat.

"I hope you realize you succeeded in making a first-class fool of yourself."

"Me?" Miranda snarled. "You, sir, succeeded in making a fool out of me long before I came to town."

Bridgett approached with plates of food. She stood at the edge of the table, uncertain whether to place them down or retreat to the kitchen.

"Regardless, you could have handled the situation with tact instead of acting like a spoiled rotten child."

"Spoiled? You know nothing about me."

"I know enough to see you blew into town and knocked me right off a ranch I had worked hard for."

"Once and for all, it was not my fault. You should have bid higher."

"I didn't have the money!" Jesse stood up, threw some bills on the table. Bridgett stepped aside to avoid toppling her plates. "I don't need this."

Miranda stood, causing Bridgett to step in the opposite direction, almost dropping everything this time.

"Where do you think you're going?" Miranda chased after him as he walked through the door.

"Away from you!" Jesse yelled over his shoulder as he threw her the truck keys. "Have fun finding your way back to the ranch."

On the sidewalk, Miranda turned to see everyone in the luncheonette watching her through the window.

"What are you looking at?" she yelled, and motioned them away with her arms. "You'll pay for this, Mr. Langtry!"

Chapter Four

Clouds of dust rose behind Miranda's pickup truck as she barreled down the ranch road full throttle. She skidded to a stop beside the back porch, just in time to hear her furniture slide forward with an incredible bang.

"Shoot!"

When the dust settled, three stunned faces appeared on the porch stairs. Mable, Beau Bradley and someone else Miranda assumed to be Aaron stood midstep, with her new buffet in hand.

Wonderful! Another audience.

She had no intention of making a scene after the one she'd made at The Magpie. While keeping a calm and level head was never her forte, the least she could do was smile pretty and be a gracious host to her guests. Especially when they were kind enough to drop off the remainder of her wares from the yard sale.

"Howdy, folks!" Miranda waved as she hopped down from the truck. "Don't mind me. I was just antiquing the furniture here. I want it to have an old, worn look to it."

As if frozen in time, they continued to stare, jaws dropped. Mable was the first to break the ice brigade.

"I heard you had quite a morning at The Magpie."

Oh, geez! It wasn't even a half hour ago! "Where'd you hear that?"

"Beau told me." Pity filled Mable's eyes. "Word travels fast in these parts, dear. Ever heard the phrase, 'faster than small town gossip'?"

It seems The Magpie lived up to its name, Miranda thought.

"But… Oh, who cares." She climbed the stairs so she could hold the door open for them. "Those people don't mean a thing to me. Let them think whatever they want."

Miranda stopped shy of the screen door and turned around.

"You know what gets me?" Miranda asked, not giving them a chance to answer. "What did I do so wrong to be treated this bad?"

After Beau introduced her to his grandson, Aaron, Miranda filled them in on The Magpie details. Full disclosure. From worrying about someone stealing her furniture to storming out of the luncheonette. Mable served a pitcher full of homemade pink lemonade and a plate full of hot cross buns while Miranda ranted about Jesse. By the time she was through, everyone agreed Jesse had been out of line. They also collectively agreed she could have maintained a little more maturity in the luncheonette.

People here sure didn't beat around the bush. At least they were honest. "Do you know I haven't even seen the entire ranch yet?" Miranda asked, changing the subject. "I don't know what those buildings are over there or where my property ends and the next one begins."

Aaron offered to show her around while Beau returned the rental trailer to the local drop-off center.

Even though she was embarrassed one of her neighbors had to give her the grand tour of her own ranch, she accepted.

Aaron surprised her with the empathy he had regarding her earlier *incident.* His jet-black hair and steel-blue eyes conveyed a bad boy image, yet he was as sweet as stolen honey.

"I knew Jesse would get himself into a heap of trouble shooting his mouth off the way he was," Aaron said. "I asked to see his fortune-telling license since he swore he knew what was going to happen to this ranch before ever meeting you."

"I think you're the exception, Aaron," Miranda said. "How many people will give me the benefit of the doubt? The damage has already been done."

"Aw, you just got off to a bad start, sweetheart." Aaron wrapped an arm around Miranda's shoulder and gave her a friendly squeeze. "Not everyone's like Bat Lady Hargrove."

Miranda almost choked on her lemonade at his reference to her incident with Charlotte. "Bat Lady?"

"We've called her Bat Lady for as long as I can remember. On account of her really having bats in her belfry. My uncle works for animal control and removes bats from her attic on a regular basis."

Aaron picked up where Mable left off the night before regarding Double Trouble's history. He told her all about the Fourth of July picnic the Carters hosted every year and how much the town would miss the tradition. He hinted she throw her own picnic and invite everyone, but Miranda would have none of it. She couldn't afford a party of that magnitude, and after the way she was treated in town today, their opinions meant nothing to her.

During their walk, Aaron explained the various outbuildings for the horses and other livestock. The chicken coop was in need of expansion. The old silo hadn't been in use for the past fifty years, could stand to come down in his opinion. The foreman's house and bunkhouse were last.

"Why that little—" Miranda bit her tongue to keep from saying more. Leave it to Jesse to make things harder on her than they needed to be. Seven cots lined the bunkhouse wall. One of which would have made a soft bed to sleep on the night before. Yet, Jesse never mentioned a single word about them being here.

Max hopped in the truck and sat between them as they drove through the upper and lower pastures. Aaron explained where her property line ran in relation to the barbed wire and mesquite fencing. From this far out on the ranch, her house was the size of a postage stamp. She knew the acreage from the closing papers, but it never meant anything to her until now. While there wasn't an abundance of farm animals, there were enough to cause her to worry about how she would manage the ranch alone.

Aaron continued the tour while Miranda sent text messages to Jonathan begging him to call her. The ranch excited her on one hand and overwhelmed her on the other. When she told Aaron her plans of opening a small boutique in town, he suggested she either hire a foreman to replace Jesse or sell the animals outright. There was no feasible way she would be able to handle the ranch and manage a store at the same time.

After she weighed her options, selling off livestock

was the best thing to do. A foreman didn't quite fit into her budget or her plans. Jesse expected to be paid and she still didn't know if she could afford Mable. The sooner the animals were gone, the sooner she could rid herself of Jesse Langtry.

Miranda was delighted she had a new friend in Aaron. *People here aren't half-bad, after all.* When he dropped her off, she tried to reach Jonathan once again. His secretary still maintained he was out of town on business. Even more reason for him to answer his cell phone. Never the one for mysteries, her patience was wearing thin with her old friend. She wanted to know why he'd kept so much from her. And did she have any other surprises coming?

"HOLD IT," MABLE CALLED OUT. "I have a few things to say to you."

"If you're about to give me an earful, don't waste your breath. I just got one from Beau." Jesse picked a coil of white cotton lead rope and a can of hoof dressing out from the bed of his truck. "He laid into me at the feed and grain after he dropped off Miranda's trailer."

"I know what you're up to," Mable snapped. "You've done enough damage. Now you're planning to make her life miserable until she's had enough and packs it in."

Jesse couldn't believe his ears. How could Mable side with a woman she hardly knew?

"We know nothing about her. For all we're concerned, she did have plans to turn Double Trouble into a housing development."

"You've got a ten-gallon mouth, you know that? Miranda's an instant outcast, no thanks to you."

"But, Mable—"

"No *buts*. You know better than this. I've known your momma and daddy all my life and they didn't raise you to act like no boll weevil," Mable said as she walked away. "Infecting doom and gloom around town and on the poor girl. I'll have no part of your little game and if I catch you spreading any more rumors, I'll tan your hide myself. And don't think you're too big for it, either."

Jesse's mouth hung open as Mable continued to berate him on her way to the house.

Out on the front porch, Miranda sat in one of her new-used rocking chairs. She ran her hands over the well-worn arms and wondered how many people had rocked in it before her. It would be perfect for lulling a child to sleep.

By this point in her life, she figured she would have had children. Five was always the number she always dreamed of. A house full of children and laughter. The dream was all but shattered when Ethan broke off their engagement two months ago.

She'd thought she loved him. Maybe at one time she did. The last thing she'd wanted to do was plan a wedding so soon after her mother's death. When she'd asked for some distance to sort her life out, instead of trying to understand, he'd criticized her for grieving over a mother who never once treated her like a daughter.

Ethan felt she should move on with her life. Leave the past in the past. A part of her knew he was right. The other part knew he wasn't the right man for her.

The breakup came as a shock at first and then a wave of relief swept over her. She drove out to her mother's grave, in Maryland, on the anniversary of her death. On the way to her apartment, she bought a lottery ticket and to her astonishment, she won. To Miranda, it was a sign from her mother to move on and start a completely new life.

Ethan returned the instant he got wind of her winning the lottery. Miranda knew he was only after her money and told him to get lost for the final time. She felt empowered. When Jonathan called and told her about the house, Miranda took it as fate and signed the papers the instant they arrived.

Something drew Miranda to Ramblewood. Yet, she hadn't quite been able to put her finger on it. Maybe it was the small town atmosphere Jonathan spoke of. Maybe it was the excitement of living somewhere new. Maybe it was the need to escape the guilt over the relief she felt when her mother died. Whatever it was, she was here now and determined to make her dreams come true.

This was her home now and she was going to do her best and make it last forever. She had no one to take care of this time except herself.

Despite the disaster at The Magpie, Miranda was rather fond of Ramblewood. The old brick buildings on Main Street reminded her of an old movie. A place where time stood still and everyone knew everyone else. A town steeped in tradition and pride. She couldn't help but fall in love with it.

Once she settled in, Miranda hoped she would find someone to share it all with. Someone to spend the rest of her life with and raise a family together. But that wasn't going to happen until she found a way to fit in. From the glares she received today, Miranda could only imagine the extent of the wreckage she once called her reputation.

Prioritize, Miranda. Animals, then reputation.

To start, she needed to sell off what livestock she had. Since Jesse made it clear he already had another job waiting for him, there was no sense dragging it out any longer. She was certain he would be able to find good homes for all of the animals. Even though she dreaded the sight of him right now, the sooner she rid herself of them, the better.

Miranda swallowed her pride, marched to the foreman's house and knocked on the door. No answer. She opened the door and peeked inside.

"Jesse?" The room was dark except for the light filtering in through the side window. "Jesse, are you in here?"

Miranda reached in and felt around for a light switch.

"Looking for something?"

Miranda's heart rose to her throat as she spun around against the doorjamb. She braced herself for the onslaught she was about to receive.

"You scared me half to death!"

"What do you want?" His jaw clenched so tight she could see it pulsate. Even though his Stetson shaded his eyes, she could feel his piercing cold stare. He reached behind her and shut the door.

"I need to talk to you about the livestock."

Miranda attempted to move away from the door and into the sunlight, but Jesse's hulking form wouldn't budge an inch. Her chest brushed his as she slid between him and the wall. The smell of sweat and horse sent her mind off in another direction. She despised this man for what he did to her, yet she was drawn to him every time he was near.

"What about the livestock?" Jesse growled.

"What? Oh, yes." Cobwebs had clouded her brain. All thoughts were on the man who stood just a hairs-breadth away. A man with a serious dislike for her. Then why did she want to pull him closer and kiss his sun-stained lips?

"Miranda?" Jesse snapped her back into reality.

Miranda stepped off the porch and steadied her nerves.

"I've thought about it, and after talking it over with Aaron, I've—"

"Aaron? Don't tell me you listened to a thing that fool had to say," Jesse said. "He's a playboy. Looking to get down those tight-fitting britches you got on."

"Hey! You don't have to be so rude."

"Me? Rude?" Jesse threw his hands in the air and walked away. "Honey, this is just part of my Texas charm. And you're a fine one to talk after the stunt you pulled at The Magpie."

"That stunt was your own creation. You master-minded the whole thing didn't you? No wonder you were so adamant about going to breakfast even though I told you I wanted to go home."

"You think I planned it? I'll take that as a compliment. Go back to where you came from. You won't make it here a month."

"I wouldn't bet on that, cowboy." Miranda followed him to the main corral.

"Okay." Jesse stopped short. "Let's bet on it."

"What are you taking about?"

"I bet—" Jesse turned toward her "—you won't last one month on this ranch."

"Oh, okay." Miranda laughed. "Some bet, there. A whole month. Wow."

"That's all it will take." Jesse hopped up to sit on the top rail of the fence.

"You're really serious?" Miranda shielded her eyes from the sun. "What are we betting?"

"The ranch."

"What?" Miranda looked skyward as she shook her head. "What do you mean 'the ranch'?"

"If you last the month, I'll leave and you'll never be bothered by me again. If I win, you sell me the ranch for what I originally bid on it. What do you say? You game or don't you think you can handle it?"

Miranda narrowed her eyes. So this was his plan. He still wanted the ranch for himself. Well, one month would be easy enough. And it would teach him a lesson not to underestimate her.

"You're on."

"And before you think you have this all figured out, there are a few ground rules." Jesse swung his legs over the fence and jumped into the corral.

"What kind of 'ground rules'?" Miranda mocked the last two words.

"You can't sell off any livestock. And you have to work like every other rancher in these parts."

Miranda opened her mouth to protest.

"And before you say the animals are too expensive, you can keep my share of the money I'll be getting tomorrow when I deliver these two horses."

Jesse attached a lead rope to one of the horses and led him to the gate.

"What do you mean, 'deliver these two horses'? Those are my horses."

"Not all of them. These two are Blueford's. I've been

training them for a while now and tomorrow they go home."

There was no way she could lose. She bought the ranch to live on, after all. Okay, so, there were a few animals to take care of. Two horses were already leaving. This would be easy.

So what was the catch? "I've got news for you, cowboy. I'm not going anywhere." Miranda held out her hand. "You have yourself a deal."

Jesse led the horse through the gate and closed out any space between her and the rest of the world. He took her hand in his and shook it firmly. The heat of his hand caused her to try to pull away.

"This is a working ranch, Miranda." Jesse ignored her attempt to break free. "It may not look like much, but there is a viable business here."

"Face facts, Jesse. You aren't staying long and I can't manage this place by myself. Once your little bet is over, the livestock goes."

"This is a ranch—those animals belong here." Jesse released her hand and led the horse toward the stables. "If you win, and you won't, but if you did, you could at least hire a foreman."

"With what money? You seem to think I am rolling in it."

"You're rolling in something." Jesse smirked.

Miranda ignored the comment and continued.

"What makes you so certain I'm loaded?" Miranda placed her hands on her hips and tapped an impatient foot.

"Look at you! All decked out in your fancy clothes. Those sure didn't come off the rack at Walmart."

"You're right. They came from Neiman Marcus."

"And you say you're not rich." Jesse dismissed her with the wave of his hand and sauntered toward the stables. "I bet you don't even know the meaning of an honest day's pay."

"You just lost your first bet," Miranda yelled to his back. "I was a sales associate."

"A sales associate?" Jesse stood where he was and stared blankly at Miranda.

"That's right, Jesse. Just about all the clothes I own are sales items which I never would have been able to afford if it wasn't for my employee discount."

"You mean you worked?" Jesse's tone softened.

"Of course I worked. I plan to work again once I get this place in order. I wasn't born with a silver spoon in my mouth, despite what you think."

"And the truck and the boots?"

"All things I bought to fit in better around here. Only it seems to have the opposite effect when it comes to you."

"A sales girl at the mall doesn't make that kind of money. There's more to it than that."

Miranda opened her mouth to tell him about the lottery when the full force of his words hit her.

"I was a bit more than a sales girl at the mall, and even if I wasn't, what is so wrong with being a sales girl, Mr. Earn an Honest Living?"

"I don't know what to say."

"You've said enough to last a lifetime." Miranda marched toward the main house. "My money is none of your concern."

"I leave with the horses first thing in the morning," Jesse called after her. Now he was the one trying to keep up with her.

"Where is this Blueford?" Miranda asked from the top step of the porch.

"Albany."

"Albany, New York?" Talk about one heck of a drive trailering two horses.

"Albany, Texas. About a four-and-half-hour drive north of here."

"Oh." Miranda felt so ignorant about the state. *Where can I buy* Texas for Dummies *or at least a bigger map?* "When do we leave?"

"We? What's this 'we'?"

Miranda cocked an eyebrow as she folded her arms in front of her.

"You certainly don't think I'm letting you out of my sight, now do you? I don't trust you. Not with the ranch on the line."

"Whatever." Jesse rolled his eyes. "You want to come, fine. Stay out of my way, though. We'll head out tomorrow."

"What time?"

"Sunup. If you're not out here by then, I'm leaving without you."

Chapter Five

"Damn roosters!" Miranda sat upright in her sleeping bag. *Who needs an alarm clock with those blasted things around?*

Still unable to reach Jonathan, she'd sent him an email last night demanding answers and outlining the events of the past few days. She knew it was too early for him to have read it yet, but she checked anyway. No new messages.

She jumped in the shower, threw on some clothes and headed out the door. Her body ached from sleeping on the floor for the second night in a row. She kicked herself for being too lazy to drag a cot in from the bunkhouse. As soon as they got back, she would buy a mattress.

Famous last words, Miranda. It's been three days now.

"Sleep well?"

Jesse snuck up behind her as she left a note on the back door for Mable. His mischievous grin told her he knew she was sore. There was no way she would give him the satisfaction of winning this round.

"Like a baby," Miranda replied, smiling. "I didn't even need a cot from the bunkhouse."

The speed in which Jesse's smile faded when he realized she knew about the extra beds amazed even her.

"I'm telling Mable." She waggled a finger at him as
she walked around the trailer, already hitched to Jesse's
truck. The horses were tied to the side.

"What are their names?"

"The chestnut is Charisma and the paint is Hawkeye." Jesse reached inside the trailer and grabbed an
armful of nylon and fleece braces.

"These are shipping boots. They protect their legs
during transport," he said as he fastened the black boots
around their lower legs. "Think you can manage to untie
Charisma?"

As Miranda moved to the left side of the horse, he
jolted and swayed sideways, almost crushing her against
the side of the trailer.

"Charisma's not fond of trailer rides," Jesse said as
he soothed the animal. "He's a little skittish. At least
you approached him from the left. You're learning."

Learning? He almost flattened me!

Charisma pulled against his harness and tie-downs
then kicked backward with both legs. Jesse quickly
snatched Miranda out of harm's way.

"Why, Jesse, I didn't know you cared," Miranda said
as she held on to him.

"Believe me, I don't." Jesse released her as if dis-
gusted with himself. "It's the load we're hauling I care
about. Not you."

Jesse's words bit into her heart. No matter what she
did or said, he insulted her in some way. It wasn't the
most ideal of situations, but couldn't he at least give
her credit for trying?

"I hate you!" The only words she could think of flew

out of her mouth before she had a chance to stop them. Not very mature.

"You hate me, huh? Want to trailer these horses alone?" Jesse mocked.

"I could if I wanted to. I am so tired of your insults. I did nothing to you. Nothing that was my fault anyway. You have a mean streak a country mile wide and a chip on your shoulder the size of Texas."

"Wowee, girl. You sure sound like a Texan. But make no bones about it, you ain't Texan. You never will be."

"That's it! Get off my ranch!" She didn't know how or where the words came from, but she'd had enough. She met every challenge and she deserved respect.

"We'll see how well you do without me." Jesse stormed off to the foreman's house, leaving her alone with the horses.

I can do this myself. I don't need him. I don't need anyone.

Miranda caught a glimpse of Jesse as he watched her from the window. Her hands trembled. She slowly began to unfasten Hawkeye's tie-downs. The horse jerked back for a brief moment and then followed her in the trailer. Inside, Miranda attempted to retie the horse the same way Jesse had. Frustrated, she yanked the tie harder than she should have, spooking the horse. Hawkeye attempted to rear. The trailer violently shifted. Miranda grabbed hold of Hawkeye's halter to steady herself. Alarmed further, the horse broke free from her grasp and knocked her to the trailer floor.

"Miranda!" Jesse pulled her to safety. "Never do that again! You'll end up killing yourself with the way you handle these horses."

Miranda ran out of the trailer while Jesse settled

the horse. He loaded Charisma while she waited in the truck, shaken and scared. She thought it would be like putting a dog in a kennel. Even though the horse was twenty times the size.

Jesse opened the door to the truck and climbed in the driver's seat.

"Are you okay? I didn't mean to—"

Throwing herself into his arms, clinging to him for dear life, Miranda knew he was the enemy and she shouldn't need him. But for the moment, all that mattered was the safety of his embrace.

Surprisingly, it felt like the most natural thing in the world.

"Shh. It's okay. Everything's okay."

Jesse enjoyed the feel of her against him. The way she fit perfectly in his arms. He didn't mean to yell at her the way he did. When Hawkeye had almost crushed her, every ounce of his soul screamed to protect her. She moved closer and Jesse fought the tremendous urge to lift her face to his and kiss away her fears.

Miranda released herself from him. Color rose high in her cheeks.

"I'm sorry." She hid her embarrassment by looking out the side window.

"So am I."

In more than one way.

Miranda continued to stare out the window without so much as a word. Since no major highway ran from Ramblewood to Albany, they took the back roads through the Hill Country. Unsure of how to ease the tension, Jesse pointed out numerous local points of interest he thought would appeal to her in each town.

Miranda was childlike in her enthusiasm over different landmarks they passed.

"What do FM and RM mean on the road signs?"

Jesse laughed. He never paid much attention to it before. It was second nature to him.

"Farm-to-Market and Ranch-to-Market," Jesse said, all too willing to give her a little lesson in Texas 101. "FM roads provide access to the rural parts of the state. You'll see RM roads when the number of ranches outnumbers farms. It goes back to old days where farmers and ranchers brought their crops and stock to market."

"That's neat," Miranda said.

Over the course of the next few hours, Miranda showered him with questions about the history of Texas. He had to admit, he loved every minute of it. She seemed genuinely eager to learn all he had to teach her. He couldn't help but admire her enthusiasm but he had to keep reminding himself this wasn't a date. She was the biggest adversary he ever had. The ranch swung in the balance.

They stopped for breakfast at a small roadside hole-in-the-wall. This time, Miranda ordered pancakes and sausage without any prodding from him. If the look on her face was any indication, she enjoyed every mouthful.

"Tell me more about this guy we're going to see."

"Blueford is an old friend," Jesse said as he took the last bite of his biscuit and gravy. "He owns the largest ranch in Shackleford County. I've trained every cutting horse he owns."

"Impressive." Miranda leaned forward. "How long does it take to train a horse?"

"Depends. Some take longer than others do. On average, eighteen months. You can only train a horse for a couple of hours a day. I like to start them when they're two and a half or three years old."

Jesse explained how training began on each horse. He was taken aback by Miranda's interest in his work. He didn't get much of an opportunity to share his passion, outside of his family. With the exception of Cole, ever since he turned down his father's last offer to join his brothers at Bridle Dance, he didn't see much of them on a social basis. Truth be told, he felt a little lonesome.

His father was as willful as he was. They both knew it and even acknowledged it on occasion, but it didn't mean either one of them would back down. Joe Langtry wanted Jesse to run the Bridle Dance Ranch alongside his brothers. He envisioned all his sons raising their families on the ranch. Now that the four Langtry boys were getting older, Joe latched on to that idea even more.

Miranda continued her Texas inquisition throughout most of their trip, not leaving much room for him to find out much about her, other than her desire to learn about the Lone Star State. Questions came from all directions on every subject. Her passion and excitement allowed him to see everything fresh and new.

Drive Carefully—Stop Wildlife Squish in Albany

The sign appeared out of nowhere. Jesse held his amusement in check until Miranda burst out laughing. Tears ran down her cheeks causing Jesse to lose control himself. Afraid he would drive the truck off the road, he pulled into the Dairy Queen parking lot.

"Wildlife squish!" Miranda wiped at her eyes. "Oh, my sides hurt. I'm sorry. I know it wasn't very funny, but it came as such a surprise."

Jesse rested his arm across the back of the bench seat and gently pushed a strand of hair away from her face. It had been a long time since he last had some humor in his life. Enjoyment was something he'd long since forgotten. Now he owed his newfound sense of it all to Miranda. The one person he should despise more than anyone else on this planet.

She looked at him with such an openness and honesty, he didn't understand how he could be so cruel to her. From the second he first laid eyes on the woman beside him, she captured a piece of his heart he was certain he'd lost forever. Once he realized his vision of beauty was the new owner, all bets were off. Miranda took from him the one thing he wanted most in this world. The chance for a life and a family, on the land that meant everything to him.

Afraid he might lose himself in a moment of weakness, Jesse proceeded through Albany's business district and into its tidy town square. They stopped at Albany's only traffic light where Miranda gasped at the impressive courthouse before her. Its limestone grandeur had astounded visitors for over a century. The sculpture garden in front of the art museum was equally as impressive, but Jesse didn't want to waste time sightseeing. The sky had an ominous look to it. He wanted to get the horses delivered to Blueford and be on their way before they had to contend with a Texas monsoon.

"There must be a million cattle out there! This place is incredible."

Through Miranda's eyes, Jesse truly saw Four Oaks Ranch for the first time. Each ranch had always been just another potential customer. He took its simple beauty for granted until he witnessed her amazement.

As they watched the swell of brown-and-white Hereford in the distance, he realized every rancher probably had the same hopes and dreams he did.

"You see out there?" Jesse pointed to a couple of men on horseback. "Those are cutting horses. They can anticipate the cattle's next move before the rider does. Those dogs are Australian cattle dogs, same as Max. In fact, Max is one of Blueford's pups."

Together as one, both man and beast danced across the land. Every step was precise yet graceful. Each horse led its rider through a perilous maze, where one false move could trigger a lethal stampede in an instant. The dogs yipped and nipped as they rounded up the stragglers left behind.

"You trained those horses?" Miranda said, unable to take her eyes off the group of riders.

"Sure did. That's Jitterbug, closest to us. Toughest darn horse to train, but worth every minute of it. He turned out to be the best one yet, outside of General Lee."

Above all else, Jesse took pride in his work. He wasn't shy about showing it, not even to her. As proud as he was, his years at Double Trouble had ended. It was time to move on. It was a shame, too. Eight horses remained in the stables and he was in the process of training seven of them. Now he'll have to start over in Abilene. Something he didn't look forward to. Unless he could convince Miranda to change her mind and sell him the ranch. Deep down, he knew that wouldn't happen anytime soon. She dug her nails in deeper and held on tighter every day.

They reached the stable area as Blueford stepped down from a sleek black gelding. He was a man of distinction in his Stetson and leather chaps. Gray temples in sharp contrast to his blue-black hair gave him a certain air of sophistication. The men shook hands and exchanged a pat on the back hug.

"And who do we have here?" Blueford tipped his hat toward Miranda.

"Miranda Archer. It's a pleasure to meet you."

"Blueford Thomas, ma'am." He took her hand in his. "Jesse, my boy, you sure know how to pick 'em."

"I didn't pick her. I got saddled with her for the time being." Miranda crinkled up her nose at his statement. "She's the new owner of Double Trouble."

"Is that so?" Blueford stepped back as if to size up her abilities to maintain a ranch. "Where are you from, pretty lady?"

"Washington, D.C., Mr. Thomas. And before you ask, no, I don't have any ranch experience. I just have a little more than I bargained for."

"Please, call me Blue." He laughed. "Honey, anyone involved with this fella here always gets more than they bargain for. He's a handful, but damn good with a horse."

"We're not involved," Jesse interjected as he walked around the trailer and began to unload the horses.

"Give him time," Blueford whispered to Miranda. "He'll come around."

"Oh, I don't think—"

"Blue, you want to give me a hand here?" Jesse cut her off before she said something she would probably regret.

Blueford whistled for one of his men to join him. They saddled the horses and rode out to a round pen. Effortless in their movements, they twisted and turned, moving each head of cattle through a chute and into a smaller corral.

Jesse watched the masterpiece he created from the top fence rail. Like a proud father watching his son's baseball game, horses had become his children. Only they didn't take the place of the void his heart was feeling of late. His dreams died when the ranch was sold. Now there was a chance he could have everything he worked for back again. Nothing would stop him this time.

"Jesse, you've outdone yourself." Blueford patted Hawkeye's neck. "I'm mighty impressed with these two. What do you think, Ty?"

Ty reined Charisma to a stop in front of Miranda.

"He's a real beaut, Blue, like the little woman here. Pardon me, ma'am." He tipped his hat and leaned toward her from his saddle. "I think you have something in your eye. Nope, it's just a sparkle."

Miranda blushed. She glanced up at Jesse and grinned. Heat rose to his face as well, but not from embarrassment. That Ty was so vain Jesse was surprised the man hadn't broken his arm patting himself on the back.

"This here is Miranda, the new owner of Double Trouble," Blueford said.

Horse and rider moved closer as he bent down to shake her hand. When he held on to her hand longer than he should have, Miranda seemed to relish the attention. *Please tell me she didn't bat her eyelashes at this guy. Time to leave. A storm is coming, after all.*

"Well, Blue, I'm glad you like them. Here are their records and feeding schedule. Same as last time. We need to get going, though."

"What's the rush, son? Stay, have some lunch and head back a little later. Give me a chance to get to know this new rancher a little better." Blueford winked at Miranda.

"Some other time. It's clouding up and I'm sure you have work to do." Jesse directed the last part straight at Ty who still clung to Miranda's hand.

"It's only getting dark because all the sunshine in the world is in this pretty lady's smile," Ty said.

"Winnie would love to see you. She'd be downright hurt if you didn't say hello." Blueford turned to Miranda. "Winnie's my better half. Now come on in the house. Bet Jesse had you up at the crack of dawn, didn't he?"

Blueford led Miranda to the main house. Jesse blocked Ty's path so he wouldn't follow. Miranda had her hands full as it was. She didn't need a cowboy with his britches on fire, hot on her heels.

I'm not jealous. I'm looking out for her. I'm not jealous.

After lunch and a quick tour of the ranch, they said their goodbyes. Jesse couldn't hightail it out of there fast enough. Ty wormed his way into a lunch invitation and managed to captivate Miranda throughout the entire meal.

"Such nice people," Miranda said as they drove away from Four Oaks. "Looks like the horses have a good home."

"Here's your money." Jesse removed a folded check out of his shirt pocket and handed it to her. "I had Blueford make it out in your name."

"What's this for?"

"Ed Carter always got a share of the training side of

things in exchange for the use of his stables and land. This is your portion and I told you I would give you my share when we made our bet."

"Keep it. I'll have to give you money anyway for feed and whatever else you need." Miranda pulled a pen from the visor and signed the check over to him. "I don't want you coming to me every time we need something, and then insulting me because I don't know what you're talking about. Use it however you see fit."

Her words stung. She made him sound like a bully. But Jesse didn't protest. He'd be a fool not to accept the money and he was tired of feeling like a fool lately.

Jesse death gripped the steering wheel at the thought of Miranda's flirtations with Ty. And the way she hung on his every word about ranch life almost sent Jesse over the edge.

"It should be me," he muttered under his breath.

"What?" Miranda asked.

"I wasn't talking to you," Jesse said, harder than he meant to.

"Fine. If you want to sit there and talk to yourself, be my guest."

It amazed him how she could push him aside without a care in the world but get downright neighborly with a total stranger. Yes, he was a stranger, too. One she had to live with, for now.

"Did I do something?" Miranda asked in a quiet voice.

"No."

"Then why the attitude?"

"I don't have an attitude!" Again, his words were harsher than he meant them to be.

"If that's not an attitude, then I don't know what is."

Dark clouds filled the sky, turning day into darkness. Rain started to fall, and within minutes, Jesse wasn't able to see past the hood of the truck. The wind whipped the trailer from side to side, as he fought to keep them on the narrow two-lane road. He knew they shouldn't have stayed at Blueford's as long as they had. Nevertheless, his old friend wouldn't have it any other way.

Lightning struck the road a few yards ahead of them. Miranda jumped toward the middle of the seat. Her body lightly brushed his, sending a chill up the back of his neck.

What on God's green earth is wrong with me? This is the enemy.

Jesse didn't understand how he could be so attracted to the woman who stole his future. Maybe it had been a long time since he'd been with a woman. He didn't have time or the patience to get involved with one now. It was time to move on, not start a relationship of any kind.

The rain came down heavier, forcing Jesse to pull off the road. Miranda questioned him without saying a word.

"I can't drive this rig any further." He leaned over the steering wheel to get a better view of the sky. "We'll stay here until it lets up."

Jesse turned the engine off and rested his head against the window. The temperature had dropped a good fifteen degrees outside. Miranda shivered. He was tempted to pull her close and keep her warm, but his senses got the better of him. He reached behind the seat, grabbed a denim shirt and handed it to her.

"Put this on."

"Thank you." She didn't look at him.

Jesse closed his eyes. She was quiet. Too quiet. He opened one eye to see her staring at him.

"Why are you looking at me like that?"

"I'm trying to figure you out."

"Nothing to figure out." Jesse closed his eyes again. "What you see is what you get."

"I don't think so." Miranda yawned. "But if you're so determined to hate me, then so be it. I can't force you to like me."

"I don't hate you, Miranda." Jesse lifted his head. "It's the circumstances I hate. In any other situation, I'd probably be asking you for a date."

Miranda didn't respond. He knew she would never be interested in a cowboy. Except maybe to play out a little nighttime fantasy. And he wasn't one for a brief fling, although they seemed to be all he ever had. A relationship with him would be beneath her. Something her folks would probably see red over.

He listened as the rain hit the roof of the truck. It didn't look like it would let up anytime soon. With good weather, they would be lucky if they made it home by midnight. The only thing they could do at this point was to find a motel and spend the night. Jesse searched for the weather on the radio. The reporter forecasted torrential rain and high wind gusts for the remainder of the night.

"What are we going to do now?" Miranda asked.

"Best we can do is find a place to hunker down for the night," Jesse said as he drove down the road at a snail's pace.

When a motel came into view, they decided to try for a couple of rooms. The parking lot was full, but the vacancy light still glowed red.

WHILE MIRANDA WAITED in the truck, Jesse checked them in at the front desk. Sheets of rain made it impossible to see more than a few feet beyond the window.

She had to laugh to herself when she thought about Jesse's reaction to Ty's friendliness toward her. If she didn't know better, she would have sworn he was jealous. She was sure that wasn't the case. He couldn't manage to be civil to her for more than ten minutes at a time.

The truck door flew open, catching Miranda off guard. Jesse hopped in, soaked to the bone. He handed her a room key.

"Thanks." She fingered the room key. "Which room are you in?"

"The same one as you, sugar." He winked. "We got the last one."

No Vacancy lit up under the motel sign.

"You're what?" Miranda hadn't considered they might share a room. "I guess it'll be okay. As long as you stay in your own bed."

"Have no fear, ma'am." Jesse touched the brim of his hat. "You'll leave with your virtue still intact."

They made a mad dash for the shelter of the overhang above the motel room doors. When they located their room, Jesse opened the door and flicked the light switch on.

"Uh-oh."

"What's wrong?" Miranda pushed her way past him. "You planned this, didn't you?"

The dimly lit room was cheap and nothing short of sleazy. Like something straight out of *Psycho.* There was a double bed in the center and two chairs on either side of a small table by the window. A television sat atop a small dresser at the foot of the bed. A four-star motel it wasn't.

A one-star motel would be an improvement over this:

"No, Miranda. I didn't plan this. I never thought to ask if the room had two beds. I'll sleep in the chairs. Somehow."

Miranda paced the entire length of the room in a few short strides. There was barely room for the furniture, let alone the two of them. She turned to look at Jesse. There was no possible way for him to sleep in those chairs. The thought of sharing a bed with him both excited and frightened her.

She didn't fear he would take advantage of the situation. In fact, she'd bet her life he would go out of his way to ignore her. That fact may have bothered her more. She alone knew they shared a common bond. They both wanted a family to call their own. The only problem was Jesse knew nothing about her. And she wasn't ready to reveal her past yet.

He would never understand how she felt when her mother died or the future she turned down with Ethan. He certainly wouldn't have any respect for her winning the lottery, not with all the nasty comments he'd made.

"Maybe we should find another place to stay."

Jesse motioned outside. "Have you seen what it's doing out there?" He closed the door behind him. "We're both tired and it's only until the storm passes. Get some sleep and we'll be on the road before you know it."

"But what about the horses back home? Who will take care of them tonight?"

"I already called Aaron when I checked in."

"Aaron? The man you love to hate? Doesn't he have his own ranch to run?"

"Not everyone owns a ranch. I may not think much of him when it comes to women, but he's the best horseman I know. Outside of myself."

That's right. No one's better than you are. Can you be any more pompous?

"You stay on your side of the room." With the door closed, the space seemed even smaller. "I smell horsey. I need a shower."

And some space.

Miranda closed the bathroom door behind her. As she braced herself against it, she surveyed the dingy tiled room. It was better than nothing. *Depends on your definition of nothing.*

Stranded in a motel room with Jesse, in the middle of nowhere, was the last place and first place she wanted to be right now. While her attraction toward him was almost unbearable, she couldn't get past his attitude. He called it "Texas charm." Miranda called it pure crap.

If he tore down the walls long enough to let her in, they might be able to become friends and work something out as far as the ranch was concerned. Then again, she was just as much at fault as he was.

While she undressed, she had to admit one thing to herself. As trashy as the motel was, sleeping in a bed would be a huge improvement over her sleeping bag on the floor. As long as the sheets were clean.

Miranda finished with her shower, stepped from the tub and wrapped an almost nonexistent towel around her. The door opened and in walked Jesse. Toothbrush in hand, he headed for the sink.

"Hey! What do you think you're doing?"

"Brushing my teeth," he said matter-of-factly. "What does it look like?"

"Looks like you barged in while I was taking my shower."

"No, I waited until I heard you turn the water off. Got you a toothbrush. They sell them at the front desk."

"How sweet of you," Miranda said sarcastically. She felt the towel start to slip and struggled to keep covered.

"I thought so." He nodded.

"Do you mind?" Miranda said as she gestured toward the door.

"Not at all. Pay no mind to me." He turned the water on and started to brush his teeth. "You don't have anything I haven't seen before."

Miranda silently fumed. How dare he lump her together with his other women. She threw caution to the wind and dropped her towel to the floor.

Jesse caught her reflection in the mirror. His mouth dropped open.

"Lord have mercy!" Jesse said with a mouthful of toothpaste. He turned to face her. "God bless Mom and Dad."

"Why, Jesse, I didn't know you cared." Miranda smiled as she gazed at the bulge forming in his jeans.

Jesse spit the toothpaste into the sink and leveled his gaze on the faucet. Miranda moved to his side so he couldn't help but get a full view of her in the mirror. Frozen, he remained bent over the sink.

"Problem, dear?"

"Not at all," he said as he rushed into the other room. "Bathroom's all yours."

Satisfied with his reaction, Miranda picked up her

towel. She wrapped it around her once again as Jesse reappeared in the doorway.

"You think you're so smart," Jesse growled as he closed the space between them. "Well, let's see how smart you really are. How about we up the ante?"

"Up...up the ante?"

His hands lingered over her arms seductively while his entire length pressed her further against the cold tile wall.

"You have to host the annual Double Trouble Fourth of July picnic." Jesse fiddled with a few strands of her hair. "And make nice with everyone in town."

Miranda closed her eyes at the feel of his warm breath against her neck.

"What are the stakes?" she asked in a husky voice that even surprised her.

"If you win, you'll have the rare satisfaction of proving me wrong." Jesse stroked her cheek with the back of his fingers. "And maybe even making a few friends in the process."

"And if I lose?" Miranda's breath was ragged.

"That's easy," he whispered in her ear. "If you lose, you'll let Ramblewood down and you'll never be accepted in this town. Even if you do win the other bet, which still stands by the way, everyone will say you were the girl who broke the Independence Day tradition."

"Why you..." Miranda snapped back to reality and tried to push him away. "That's a little dramatic, don't you think?"

Jesse braced himself on either side of her so Miranda couldn't escape. Miranda kicked him in the shin with her bare foot causing them both to wince.

Oh, that hurt!

"Next time, put shoes on." Jesse smirked. "This is Texas, sugar. We are steeped in tradition. You let them down and they will never forget it."

"Fine, I'll do it." Miranda attempted to hold out her hand to shake on it. "Fourth of July picnic it is."

Jesse's mouth crashed down upon hers. All too quick to comply, she tasted the urgency of his kiss along with a hint of peppermint as he parted her lips with his tongue. He pulled her tighter to him. Animosity forgotten, Miranda wrapped her arms around his neck, savoring the feel of his hardened form against her.

He broke the kiss as fast as he began it.

"I thought sealing this deal with a kiss would make it more official." He walked to the door and turned to face her. "Oh, and don't forget your towel, sugar."

Miranda looked down. Her towel had fallen to the floor sometime during their kiss. That breathtaking kiss.

Chapter Six

Sprawled across the bed, Jesse propped himself up on his elbows while he watched the local news. Snacks and sodas were laid out on the table. A vending machine raid must have occurred while she was in the shower.

"Finished in the bathroom?" he asked, not looking up.

"Yes."

Jesse rose from the bed and walked past Miranda, avoiding eye contact. He shut the bathroom door behind him.

The roughness of his evening stubble lingered against her cheek. Miranda had been disappointed the kiss ended so abruptly. Sitting on the bed, she popped open a can of soda. He even thought to make it diet. Maybe he did pay attention to her grumblings about her weight after all. *Either that or he thinks I'm fat.*

The coolness of the can against her lips replaced the warmth of Jesse's kiss. The television drowned out the rain pounding down on the roof. Heavy from exhaustion, her eyes slowly closed out the day's events.

SUN STREAMED THROUGH the window where the curtains didn't quite meet all the way. She snuggled deeper into

Jesse's chest, his arm tightening around her as he kissed the top of her head.

Miranda's eyes flew open. She patted the area next to her and shot upright. Her hand stopped shy of his... *Oh, no!*

"Get out of my bed!" She pushed him away and his body thudded against the floor. Surprised at her strength, Miranda peered over the edge of the bed.

Whoops!

Jesse's head popped up and startled her.

"What was that for?" Jesse asked as he shook off the night's sleep.

"What were you doing?" Miranda rose to her knees, hands on her hips. He had better come up with a good answer for this one. "You told me you would sleep in the chair."

Jesse hauled himself on the bed. Without a word, he glared at her.

"I didn't hurt you did I?" Miranda questioned.

"As if you could," Jesse shot back. "We both knew I couldn't sleep in those tiny chairs. I didn't think you would attack me for sharing a bed with you."

"Sharing a bed is one thing. Taking advantage of me is another."

"Get over yourself, will you?" Jesse rose before her, clad in nothing but a pair of boxer briefs. A pair he filled out rather well.

"*You* cozied up to *me*. I'm a man, Miranda. Who am I to refuse your utmost desires? I'd be a fool to resist your affections."

Affections?

"You thought I was coming on to you?" How dare he be so presumptuous? She may be attracted to him, but it didn't mean she'd sleep with him. *Well, at least not so soon.*

Jesse reached for his clothes and boots and tugged them on. "Get yourself together and let's go. I'll meet you outside."

He snatched the room key from the table and left her alone. What happened? Last night they'd argued in the bathroom and then this morning she found herself wrapped up in his arms. It was a feeling she enjoyed more than she cared to admit.

ONCE THEY WERE BACK at the ranch, Jesse and Miranda went their separate ways. A word didn't pass between them the entire drive home. Instead, they both silently stewed over the other. Mable greeted Miranda on the porch with a wary smile.

"How was your trip, child?"

"Interesting, to say the least."

Miranda and Mable shared a good laugh over Jesse's jealousy of Ty and Jesse's unfortunate, sudden removal from bed that morning.

"You're going to be the death of him."

"Me?" Miranda smirked. "What did I do?"

"It's written all over the boy's face. As much as he wants this ranch, he gave up on the idea the day he found out it was sold."

"What are you trying to say?" Miranda asked, not sure she wanted to hear the answer.

"He's stayed on for you." Mable beamed. "I do believe the boy is smitten with you."

"I'm flattered you would think so." Miranda wanted this topic of conversation over with fast. "But I think you're mistaken. There may be a sexual attraction on his part, but that's about it. He's staying because of our bet."

After a hot shower, Miranda headed into town with Mable to finally pick out a bed. Mable suggested a bite to eat at The Magpie. Famished, Miranda accepted with only slight hesitation. After the other day, she wasn't sure she would be welcome there ever again.

Plus, she wanted to nail down Mable's salary now that she was almost finished moving back into the guest cottage. With Jesse's bet, she needed Mable's assistance now more than ever. What's one more adjustment to her finances? She'd been adjusting all her life.

A few people stared as they walked through the luncheonette door. Mable shot each one a warning glance as if to intimidate them to be on their best behavior. Miranda giggled. It was funny to think of Mable as her bodyguard.

"Afternoon, ladies." Bridgett sat two glasses of water on the table. "How are you doing, Miranda? Mable?"

Miranda breathed a sigh of relief. At least the woman didn't hold a grudge. Although, Miranda had a feeling Ramblewood would remember her little scene for a long time to come. Especially considering how fast Beau and Aaron got wind of it. Mable said small town gossip traveled fast. She wasn't kidding.

Lunch at The Magpie went better than expected. She met Maggie Dalton, the owner of the luncheonette, a sweet woman who doted on every customer as if they were family.

The brave and the curious ventured over to their table. Mable introduced her as the new owner of Double Trouble as if there was anyone in town who didn't already know that. Mable strategically stressed the fact

Miranda was new in town. She even acted as if she had arrived that day. It gave Miranda a clean slate and a suggestion to her neighbors to do the same.

Everyone in the luncheonette knew everyone else. The people at one table joined in the conversation at the next. Before long, the entire place was talking about the same thing. It was a fun, homey atmosphere Miranda thought only existed on television.

After lunch, with Mable's pay settled, Miranda purchased a mattress and box spring from Mayfield's. Not wanting to wait another day for its delivery, she had the store load it in the bed of her truck.

The two women struggled unloading the bed when they arrived home. Jesse offered his assistance, but they insisted they were capable of handling things themselves. Once inside the house, getting the darned thing up the stairs was another matter altogether.

The narrow stairs that led off the kitchen accommodated the mattress. However, there was no way the box spring would make the sharp turn at the top.

"How in the world did people ever get anything up to the second floor?" Miranda asked as she swiped the sweat off her forehead with her arm. "Were people really small, with tiny furniture a hundred years ago when this house was built?"

Mable struggled with her end of the box spring. "This is insane, Miranda. We need Jesse."

"Maybe if we try the stairs in the living room." She wasn't about to ask Jesse for help. He wouldn't be around for much longer—one month was the deal and she was determined to win. She might as well start doing things without his help now.

"I am too old to fight with this bed any longer."

Mable brushed her hands together. "And my nephew will be here soon with what's left of my furniture."

"Okay, okay. I'll go up and get the bed frame together in the meantime. Let me know when Jacob gets here and I'll come help you."

"Don't you worry about me, child," the woman said. "You have plenty of your own work to do around here."

The iron bed went together with relative ease. It was a handsome antique. Beau said it had been in his attic for years. Now if she could only get the rest of the bed up the stairs, she'd be in business.

Stretching out her back, Miranda caught a fresh breeze at the open window. She gazed out to see Jesse, who stood in the middle of the corral, a horse circling him. A length of rope tied to the horse in one hand and a whip in the other. The whip cracked through the air at the poor defenseless animal.

Enraged, Miranda flew down the stairs and through the kitchen, startling Mable.

"Slow down, child."

"Jesse's hurting that horse!"

Before Mable could respond, Miranda was outside. She swung the corral gate wide-open and stormed into the center.

"Put down that whip!" Miranda ordered.

Startled, the horse reared and tried to bolt, almost dragging Jesse behind him. He fought to regain control. Miranda watched as the animal twisted and kicked to break free.

"Close the gate!" Jesse fought to hold on to the rope with both hands.

"Give me the whip now!" Miranda shouted.

"You have no idea what you're talking about. Get out of here!"

"I will not let you abuse that animal."

Jesse lost his grip as the horse broke free and charged toward the opening.

"Loose horse!" Jesse yelled.

Miranda ran to the side of the corral. The horse tore past her. Jesse ran to the stables and flew out of them, bareback on General Lee.

She watched through the clouds of dust General Lee's hooves kicked up. The horse ran down the drive and headed toward the main road. *Oh, no!* It wasn't a busy road, but just the same. She didn't want to see anything happen to the animal.

A large blue pickup drove into the ranch. Aaron! He cut the wheel and blocked the horse's path. He jumped out and pulled rope from the bed of the truck. Swinging the lariat above his head, he looped the horse's neck. Jesse rode up and snatched it from his hands. He reined the horse to a complete stop and tied the rope off to his saddle horn. On foot, Aaron caught up and soothed the horse.

"You better turn tail and run before Jesse gets ahold of your hide."

Mable stood behind her, her hands on her hips and her foot tapping madly.

"I didn't do anything! He had a whip and—"

"He was lunging," Mable interrupted. "It's a form of training."

"But—"

Mable didn't give her a chance to finish her sentence. "The whip never touched that horse. It's the sound that makes the horse move forward."

Miranda watched Aaron and Jesse walk the horse to the stables. She could have sworn he was whipping the horse.

Aaron stopped before the stable entrance. Jesse headed straight for her. Thin lines formed deep across his brow, arms close to his sides, fists clenched.

"Stay away from the horses from now on," Jesse growled as he advanced. "You cause trouble every time you're around."

Miranda quickly moved behind Mable, putting her between the two of them for protection. Mable held up her hands to calm Jesse.

"Take it easy, Jesse," Mable pleaded. "She didn't know."

"Jesse," Aaron called with a hint of trepidation in his voice.

Ignoring them both, Jesse glared over the top of Mable's head at Miranda.

"I mean it. You stay away from them."

"I'm sorry," Miranda said. "From where I stood it looked like you were hurting him."

"You must not think much of me, then." Jesse clenched and unclenched his fists. "What if the horse got hit by a car? He could have been killed and so would whoever was driving."

Miranda paled. She hadn't thought that far ahead. All she wanted to do was protect the horse.

"I didn't know" was all she mustered.

"Go back to wherever you came from!" Jesse stomped to the stables, passing Aaron on his way out. "Useless woman."

What? The words registered as soon as they left his mouth. No one called her useless and got away with it. She had enough of that with her mother. Claire always said Miranda would never amount to anything. Working in a department store was a *useless job* in her mother's book.

Miranda stormed into the stables after him. Aaron caught her arm, stopping her.

"Let him cool off, Miranda. If you go in there now, you may not come out alive."

Miranda broke from his grasp.

"Did you hear what he called me? I am not useless!"

Aaron put an arm around Miranda's shoulder and led her away from the stables.

"Let's go inside and you can tell me what happened."

Miranda moved away. She didn't want to be pacified or coddled. She wanted to be mad. Mad at Jesse, mad at Jonathan for not returning her calls, and mad at herself for being so stupid and assuming Jesse was hurting the horse.

In the kitchen, Miranda couldn't bear to look at Mable. She pulled her cell phone from her back pocket and tried to reach Jonathan again. Voice mail, as she expected. With Aaron and Mable watching her, she opted not to leave the heated message burning her lips and hung up the phone.

"Grab an end." Miranda picked up an end of the box spring. "We're getting this upstairs even if it kills us."

Without a word, Aaron lifted the other end and after a half hour of the two of them pushing and swearing, they finally got it up the narrow staircase and onto the bed frame.

"Who designs stairs two feet wide with a turn large enough only to accommodate an infant?" Miranda said as she slid down the wall of the bedroom and sat on the floor.

"Oh, I don't know," Aaron responded. "I'd say a toddler could get through there."

Miranda faced Aaron sitting on the box spring and started to laugh. The whole situation she had gotten herself in was so absurd. He reached out and helped her to her feet.

"Come on. Let's get the mattress on, so you have some place to sleep tonight."

Once the bed was together, Miranda removed a set of new sheets from a bag on the floor. They made the bed together, play fighting with the fitted sheet.

"Good thing I bought a double bed. I'd hate to go up those stairs with a queen size."

Aaron surveyed the room. "Got a bedspread? Or pillows?"

"My pillows are downstairs with my sleeping bag." Miranda motioned toward the hall. "I'll pick up a bedspread once I get this room painted."

"Sounds good."

"What do you think, Aaron?" Miranda sat on the bed and patted a place beside her. "How does a nice pale yellow with white trim sound to you?"

"I can see that in here. Hanson's Hardware will have everything you need."

"Hanson's Hardware?"

"It's on the corner of Main and Shelby. We don't have any of those supercenters for about fifty miles. It's Hanson's or nothing. But don't worry, he's more than fair on his prices and you won't get the personal service at one of those fancy places that you will at Hanson's."

Miranda was grateful for the few friends she'd made

in Ramblewood. Now if she could only make a few more, she might feel a little more secure. What didn't make her feel too secure right now was Jesse. Their bet loomed over her like a bad dream the morning after. How could she hold up her end of the bet if the horses were off-limits? Wait a minute. They were *her* horses and she could spend as much time around them as she wanted!

Miranda proceeded to tell Aaron all about both bets, minus the kiss they shared to seal the deal. She touched her fingers to her lips, remembering the hunger Jesse had possessed. And how disappointed she'd felt when the kiss quickly ended.

"Uh-oh," Aaron said. "Looks like a little more happened last night than you've let on."

"Nothing happened." Miranda could kick herself for her little trip down memory lane. "We rented a room and went to sleep. Nothing else."

"Sure, darlin'. And pigs have wings."

Aaron seemed amused by the entire situation. Although not surprised, which bothered Miranda to some degree. Was this what Jesse did? Pick up women and seduce them as some sort of a hobby? Somehow, Miranda doubted it to be the case. Either that or she was trying to convince herself into thinking she was in some way special to him.

"All right, go ahead and ask," Aaron said as he rose from the bed.

"Ask what?"

"You're wondering about the bad blood between me and Jesse."

"I don't get it." Miranda opened a few bags and started to unpack.

"He claims I stole his girl," Aaron continued. "I can assure you, I never knew he was interested in her. As you can see, she isn't around now. We both lost."

"I see." Miranda added a few more things to the closet and closed the door. "How long ago was this?"

"Ten years." Aaron laughed. "Jesse sure does hold a grudge."

"How childish." Miranda made her way downstairs. "Jesse has some growing up to do."

"Is that so?" Jesse stood at the bottom.

Miranda was surprised to see him, but she wasn't fazed, either. She walked past him as if he wasn't there. If he found her so useless as a human being, she couldn't be bothered acknowledging him.

"So you said Hanson's will have everything I need?"

"It's right next to the beauty parlor on Main Street. You can't miss it." Aaron shifted his feet. His discomfort around Jesse was obvious. "I better head outside."

"You never said why you came here today," Miranda noted, following him to the porch.

"Just being neighborly, ma'am." Aaron tipped his hat and nudged her with his elbow. "I wanted to see if Jacob and Mable needed any help. Looks like I got here in the nick of time."

"You sure did." They watched a white pickup loaded to the hilt pull down the ranch drive. "Thanks for the help with the box spring."

"Happy to help." And with that, Aaron took off.

Miranda felt the heat from Jesse's glare burn through her. When she turned, she found herself slamming righty into Jesse's chest.

"Stop acting like a jealous fool and get out of my way!" Miranda ordered.

"Jealous. Over him?" Jesse laughed. Before he could continue, Miranda held up her hand to stop him.

"Aaron told me what happened between the two of you. Ten years ago."

"So?" Jesse followed her through the kitchen.

"Forget it. There is no sense in explaining anything to you. He's just a friend."

"Yeah, some friend he'll turn out to be. He's only after one thing."

"That's it." Miranda had enough of his attitude for one day. "Get out of my house and help Jacob."

"What did I do?" Jesse asked, surprised.

Should I make a list? She took a long hard look at the man before her. It was futile to continue to fight with him. Neither one of them ever won.

"Look, I'm sorry for earlier. I didn't know. Just… just leave me alone right now."

"We have a deal you know?" Jesse stood his ground. "I'm not doing all the work around here."

"Jesse, stop." Miranda turned her back to him. "Please go. I'll be out in a minute."

"Fine. But tomorrow you meet me at the stables at 7:00 a.m., sharp." Jesse left Miranda alone in the kitchen.

"What on earth?"

Jesse came out from the foreman's house and saw Miranda on the front porch sanding down the furniture she had bought from Beau.

"Well, I'll be. She's actually going to refinish the stuff."

Not wanting her to know he was the least bit interested in her handiwork, Jesse went inside and watched her through the window. Again, he found himself feeling bad for the way he treated her earlier. Nevertheless, the woman needed to learn a thing or ten about horses before she got herself in a whole heap of trouble.

Trouble. Trouble like Aaron. As much as he detested the man on a personal basis, he was glad he was able to take care of the ranch last night. Aaron was the best man for the job, especially on such short notice, and Jesse knew Aaron needed the money. But Jesse sure didn't want Aaron to have the remote chance of taking advantage of Miranda. He was certain she never wrestled with a cowboy before. Especially one with Aaron's reputation.

Why he cared if she was with Aaron was beyond him. In another month, she wouldn't be his problem anymore. She could run off with Aaron Bradley for all he cared. Get married, have a couple of kids.

The bitter taste of bile that rose in his throat caught him off guard. He cursed himself aloud for last night's kiss. It never should have happened, yet he wished it lasted longer. If he had a sliver of common sense, he'd keep his distance from her.

There was no getting around it, Jesse had his work cut out for him. Miranda had dug her heels in deep and wasn't giving in anytime soon. He hoped the added stakes of the picnic would overwhelm her to the breaking point. At least that was the plan.

The tailgate of her truck was open and Jesse noticed some paint cans and supplies in the bed. Flats of flowers and bags of potting soil were nearby on the ground. By the sound of things coming from the porch, he could only assume she bought a mess of power tools while she was at it.

No, this definitely wouldn't be a cakewalk, but at least he had the foresight to bring an unsuspecting Mable in to help with the house and the chickens, while he wore Miranda down with the outside work and showed her just how over her head she was. That is if he could keep her away from Aaron.

Jesse had worked up a list of things she needed to do around the ranch. When Double Trouble was fully staffed, running things went smoothly. Now that it was just the two of them, three counting Mable, there was plenty of work to go around.

A few hours later, when Jesse was leaving for Slater's Mill to meet up with some friends, Miranda was still hard at work on the porch. Pages from a magazine were taped to the railing. The girl had gumption.

Mable was prodding her to come in for dinner, but Miranda wasn't having none of it. Mable was actually waving a plate of food under the woman's nose, which seemed to break Miranda down. No one could resist the woman's cooking.

At the bar Jesse caught up with a few of the locals and put to bed the rumors he had started about Miranda before she arrived in town. Common sense told him to set the record straight while another part of him wanted the whole town to hate her. Jesse knew he'd been in the wrong. Yet he still wished she would pack up and leave. Give him back his ranch and the part of his heart she already grabbed ahold of. The last thing he needed was to fall in love with the enemy.

With his plan set in motion, Jesse headed back to the ranch to finish what chores he could before it was time to turn in. From the driveway, Jesse spotted Miranda and Mable kneeling in the dirt in front of the farmhouse. She'd planted the flowers she'd bought earlier. Mable waved but Miranda never bothered to look up.

The woman never stops! Then again, maybe it was his fault. He pretty much told her he wouldn't give her any time to herself. She did what she could when the time allowed. By the looks of things, she wasn't about to let him interrupt her. Not even long enough to wave hello.

He climbed out of his truck, peeking into the bed of hers. It was empty and freshly hosed out. With the little he knew about Miranda, he was willing to bet she would start painting the inside of the house tonight.

When he reached the porch, he ran his hand over the freshly sanded furniture. Not a trace of stain or paint remained. There were a few links of chain on top of the sideboard. What did she plan to do? Chain her furniture down so no one would steal it?

He had his own work to worry about. Miranda still hadn't mentioned how she would pay him, even though he made it very clear a few days ago he wouldn't work for free. It would be a topic up for debate tomorrow.

Jesse saddled General Lee and rode out to the north pasture. He had to move the few heads of cattle they had within the next day or so. Though only used to train the cutting horses, he needed to keep them healthy. A move to a new pasture was in order. Selling the animals was the one thing he was glad he stopped Miranda from doing. If they were gone, you might as well tear down the entire place. They were the heart and soul of Double Trouble.

By the time he arrived home, it was well after dark. There was Miranda, still working away on her furniture. The porch light was aglow and so was a brand-new bug zapper. The woman thought of everything.

Still guilty for the way he treated her, he decided to bury the hatchet. Miranda was studying the dresser as he climbed the porch stairs. She'd painted a light coat of whitewash over the piece.

"I thought I had until seven tomorrow morning," she said without looking up again.

"I just wanted to see how you were." Jesse regretted his words. It sounded as if he was checking up on her. It was more curiosity if it was anything.

"I'm fine, Mr. Langtry. You can go back to whatever it was you were doing."

Jesse sat on the first step and watched Miranda methodically paint and then rub off certain areas she just brushed.

"What does that do?" Jesse asked, transfixed by her actions.

"It gives the furniture a more distressed look, like this." She untaped a magazine page from the porch railing and handed it to him. "Once it dries I'll sand it off in some areas and hit others with the chain over there."

"If you wanted the worn look, why didn't you leave it the way it was?" Jesse never would understand a woman's mind. "It was pretty worn-looking before."

"Because I wanted it to be white." Miranda still didn't look up at him. She kept her attention focused on the dresser.

Jesse continued to watch her work. The way her delicate wrist moved in one fluid motion over the top of the dresser like a ballet dancer. The way she stepped back and examined the piece after each brush stroke.

The way she was oblivious to the fact he was sitting there staring at her.

"Where's Mable?" he asked, surprised she wasn't out here, either helping or trying to stuff a piece of pie in Miranda's mouth.

"Inside."

"Mind if I go in?" Jesse knew he wasn't about to get any more of a conversation out of her tonight.

"Be my guest."

Upstairs Jesse found Mable taping off the woodwork in Miranda's room. She shook her head when she saw him and made that *tsk tsk* sound he'd hated so much when he was younger.

"The girl has plans to get up tomorrow morning and paint this room before she joins up with you. She would have stayed up half the night taping if I hadn't offered to help."

Amazed, Jesse began to realize how bound and determined Miranda was to make this place hers. He grabbed a roll of tape and started on the other side of the room.

"No sense in you doing all of this." Jesse tore off a strip of blue painters tape and applied it to the baseboard. "Especially since this is my fault."

Mable handed him the tape. "You're right." She walked to the door. "She told me all about your bets. I warned you. She has my full support on the picnic and I'll make sure she has other people to help her, too. Oh, and shelves need to go in the closet tonight. Would you mind?"

Jesse figured he deserved the cold tone in Mable's voice. Screws, a level and a drill were on the floor next to the closet. He opened the closet door. Pencil marks on the wall already indicated where Miranda planned to mount the shelving brackets. Ambition was one thing. Trying to squeeze all of this in before daybreak was another. A day only had so many hours.

Miranda cleared her throat behind him. He turned to see her standing with a paint can in one hand and a brush in the other.

"What are you doing in here?"

"Helping you."

"I don't need your help. Thanks, anyway." She sat the can of paint on the worn hardwood floor and took out a tape measure. She checked the dimensions of the inside of the closet, wrote them down on a pad and headed downstairs.

About a half hour later, she returned with an armful of cut wood.

"Miranda," he said as he took them from her arms and stacked them on the floor. "I need your help and you need mine."

She mulled over his words for a minute. "Fine. You put up the shelves and I'll finish taping the room."

Without another word between them, they worked side by side for the next few hours. Jesse didn't understand why he was helping Miranda. He liked to think it was an apology of some sort. But the truth of the matter was, he enjoyed being near her. By midnight, they finished the minor projects in the room. All the room needed was paint.

MIRANDA AWOKE AT FIVE the next morning, after a night of pure heaven in her new bed. *I think that was better than sex.* Well, maybe not. Then again, it had been so long she couldn't remember. All she knew for certain was it sure beat sleeping on the floor. She bounded out of bed and immediately cracked open a can of pale yellow paint. She managed to paint the walls and the closet with not much time to spare before she had to meet Jesse. She took a quick shower, ran down the stairs. At the bottom, Mable stood holding a cup of coffee and a warm blueberry muffin.

Miranda smiled. "Thanks, Mable. You really are heaven sent, you know it?"

She leaned her hip against the kitchen counter as she finished her coffee. Five years into the future, Miranda envisioned herself baking sugar cookies with her daughter. She inhaled deeply, almost smelling them. Her husband at the table reading the morning paper. The day ahead of them as a family. Then the sound of her cell phone ringing jolted her back to reality.

Jonathan's number appeared on the caller ID. Finally!

"You better start explaining yourself, buster." All she heard was static. "Hello? Jonathan?"

"He can't win the bet." Jonathan's voice broke through the static and then the call was disconnected.

"I guess that means he got my email." Miranda looked at the phone in her hand, willing it to ring again. "But what does he care about the bet?"

Jonathan's phone went straight to voice mail when she tried calling him back. "He finally got the nerve to pick up the phone and he calls me from a crappy signal area."

Outside, Jesse had saddled two horses and was waiting for her.

"I'll ride General Lee. You can ride Lone Star," Jesse said as he nuzzled the paint horse.

Miranda remained frozen where she stood. Yesterday's words echoed in her head. Every time she got near a horse, disaster struck.

"Lone Star's the tamest horse I've got," Jesse said as he coaxed Miranda closer.

Still frozen in place she stared at the magnificent beast before her. Lone Star peered around at her, twitching his ears.

"How about a refresher course on horsemanship first," Jesse offered. "It should ease your mind."

Miranda nodded.

"Remember, approach from the left. Never sneak up on him. Let him see you first."

Jesse continued with the riding lessons on a saddle stand and after an hour, Miranda finally built up the nerve to attempt to ride Lone Star. Once horse and rider were acquainted, he lifted her into the saddle and let her walk around the smaller corral. When she felt a little more secure, they rode into the north pasture to check on the cattle.

Jesse explained he would be moving cattle to another pasture tomorrow. While he didn't expect Miranda to pitch in, he gave her the courtesy of knowing he was bringing in a few hands to help him and they would be milling about.

Mable had packed a lunch and given it to Jesse before Miranda came downstairs. They found a quiet place to eat under the shade of some oaks. Jesse tied General Lee to a nearby tree. Miranda remained atop Lone Star.

"Are you coming down?"

Miranda shook her head.

"Why not?"

"I don't think I can. I lost all feeling in my rear end about two hours ago."

Jesse laughed and helped Miranda off her horse. Had he forgotten she never rode before? Miranda walked, legs bowed, to a tree. Her thighs quivered as she eased herself down.

"Leave me here," Miranda said as she closed her eyes. "Come back for me tomorrow."

"No way." Jesse tried to hide a triumphant smile. "You'll get used to it. By the end of the week you'll be riding like a pro."

Miranda's eyes shot open.

"You mean I have to do this again?"

"Sure." Jesse handed her a neatly wrapped turkey on rye sandwich. "Every day we need to ride out and check the cattle. Fences need to be checked. Troughs and mineral feeders need to be filled. Soon you'll be riding out here on your own."

"I don't think—"

"You better start thinking." Jesse sat down beside her. "What will you do if you win this bet, Miranda? All of this will be your responsibility. Then what will happen? It's not a lot of cattle, but you have to know what you're doing all the same."

Miranda didn't answer him. Instead, she ate her lunch in silence. She didn't see much sense in keeping the cattle after she won. None of this would be a factor.

"Ready to head out?" Jesse repacked General Lee's saddlebags.

"A little help over here?" Miranda attempted to climb into the saddle with little success.

"My pleasure, ma'am," Jesse said as he tipped his hat. On Miranda's first bounce in the stirrup, he firmly placed a hand on either butt cheek and hoisted her up.

Miranda shot him a look. "I said a little help, Mr. Langtry. Not help yourself."

Back at the stables, Jesse explained two of the horses required medication on a daily basis. He taught her how to grind their pills in a small electric coffee bean grinder, mix in molasses and then add the concoction to an oral syringe. Fascinated, Miranda even offered to assist him when he administered them.

Jesse explained feeding schedules and the signs of colic she needed to watch for. He went over daily grooming routines and saddle maintenance. Overwhelmed, Miranda didn't know how she would remember it all. Her head started to spin with the overload of information he was tossing at her.

The sun was low in the western sky when they heard the sound of a loud bell.

"What was that?" Miranda asked.

"The dinner bell. What else?"

Miranda had noticed the triangle shape bell on the porch, but she figured it was the remnants of a broken wind chime. Heaven knows why Mable would start ringing the blasted thing. No one else was there except Jesse and her.

"Tradition," Jesse said, answering her unasked question. "Things are finally returning to normal around here."

The aroma of country-fried steak made her realize how hungry she was when she walked into the kitchen. They ate as Miranda told Mable all about their day. Jesse laughed at her enthusiasm, but frowned the moment she said she'd had fun.

"What's wrong, Jesse?" Miranda questioned sarcastically. "Is there a little flaw in your plans to drive me off the ranch?"

Jesse kept his head down, cut up his steak and ignored her.

"You thought I'd whine all day didn't you?"

"I figured you would enjoy it, once you got the feel of things."

Miranda knew it was a lie. She wished Jesse truly felt that way. Life would be easier if she didn't have to keep looking over her shoulder all the time to see if he was about to stab her in the back. Just the same, she was sure he felt like someone stabbed him in the back when he lost the ranch. Maybe his heart suffered the most damage instead.

"Mable, I came up with some great ideas for the picnic. Jesse and I ate lunch in the most perfect spot for some relay races for the kids. We can have a hayride out there."

"See, child? Planning this shindig is half the fun."

Despite her aches in places she didn't know she could ache, Miranda enjoyed the time she spent with him today. For the most part, he was civil and left the snide remarks at home. He had an endearing side to him. One she wanted to get to know better.

"I think you've done enough for one day." He rose and helped Mable clear the table.

Do I need my hearing checked?

"You mean I have the rest of the night off?"

"Yep. I'm giving you a chance to work on the house instead of staying up until the wee hours of the morning. But only because you have a long day ahead of you tomorrow."

Jesse excused himself and went to sit on the porch.

Miranda offered to clean the kitchen but Mable would have no part of it.

Miranda put the finishing touches on her distressed dresser. With Jesse's help, the three of them managed to get it up the living room stairs, which weren't much wider than the kitchen staircase.

Miranda almost dropped her end of the dresser when she saw her room. The trim molding was bright white. The tape removed. A white coverlet with antique lace throw pillows completed the bed. Lace curtains hung from the windows and two little white end tables sat on either side of the bed.

"It suits you, doesn't it?" Mable beamed.

"Oh, I love it!" Miranda hugged her friend as she continued to look around the room. "How did you do all of this?"

"The lace I had for years. I never had a use for it until now. The coverlet was something I picked up for you, as a gift," Mable stressed. "Beau stopped by this morning and said he had these two white antique tables he wanted to give you as a housewarming present and while he was here, we painted the trim."

The room was everything she envisioned. Quaint, cozy and tranquil. It was something out of a magazine. It was her dream bedroom. And it was perfect.

"I don't know what to say." *These people barely know me.* "Thank you so much. It's exactly how I pictured it would look."

"Now you have one room completed in your house. A room for you *alone*." Mable nudged Jesse in the ribs to get her point across.

"I'm going to shower and change real quick, so I can ride over and thank Beau."

"He'll be here in about an hour. I invited Beau and Aaron over for coffee and peach pie."

Out of the corner of her eye, Miranda saw Jesse's face fall.

Chapter Seven

Miranda opened her eyes and looked around her new room. Sunlight streamed through the window. Combined with the pale yellow walls, the room radiated such warmth. She would give anything to curl up and sleep for another couple of hours.

The kindness and help from Mable and her new neighbors took Miranda off guard. She wouldn't have gotten such support in Washington, even from people that she knew. Double Trouble was starting to feel like a home with her bedroom finished. Now she had the rest of the house to tackle, along with whatever Jesse threw her way.

She was not about to lose the bet and give up the ranch—he would be the one sent packing.

Yesterday put Miranda a little more at ease. She felt more comfortable around the horses, even though she figured Jesse was trying to scare her more than teach her. Those big horned cattle were another thing altogether. Even though Aaron told her they were gentle giants, she didn't want to meet up with one of them in the middle of the night.

Miranda flung the covers off and threw her legs over the side of the bed.

Send For
2 FREE BOOKS
Today!

I accept your offer!

Please send me two free
Harlequin American Romance®
novels and two mystery
gifts (gifts worth about $10).
I understand that these books
are completely free—even
the shipping and handling will
be paid—and I am under no
obligation to purchase anything, ever,
as explained on the back of this card.

154/354 HDL FS6X

Please Print

FIRST NAME

LAST NAME

ADDRESS

APT.#   CITY

STATE/PROV.   ZIP/POSTAL CODE

Visit us online at
www.ReaderService.com

Offer limited to one per household and not applicable to series that subscriber is currently receiving.

Your Privacy—The Reader Service is committed to protecting your privacy. Our Privacy Policy is available online at www.ReaderService.com or upon request from the Reader Service. We make a portion of our mailing list available to reputable third parties that offer products we believe may interest you. If you prefer that we not exchange your name with third parties, or if you wish to clarify or modify your communication preferences, please visit us at www.ReaderService.com/consumerchoice or write to us at Reader Service Preference Service, P.O. Box 9062, Buffalo, NY 14269. Include your complete name and address.

© 2011 HARLEQUIN ENTERPRISES LIMITED. ® and ™ are trademarks owned and used by the trademark owner and/or its licensee. Printed in the U.S.A. ▲ Detach card and mail today. No stamp needed. ▲ H-AR-S13

The Reader Service—Here's how it works: Accepting your 2 free books and 2 free gifts (gifts valued at approximately $10.00) places you under no obligation to buy anything. You may keep the books and gifts and return the shipping statement marked "cancel." If you do not cancel, about a month later we'll send you 4 additional books and bill you just $4.49 each in the U.S. or $5.24 each in Canada. That is a savings of at least 14% off the cover price. It's quite a bargain! Shipping and handling is just 50¢ per book in the U.S. and 75¢ per book in Canada.* You may cancel at any time, but if you choose to continue, every month we'll send you 4 more books, which you may either purchase at the discount price or return to us and cancel your subscription.

*Terms and prices subject to change without notice. Prices do not include applicable taxes. Sales tax applicable in N.Y. Canadian residents will be charged applicable taxes. Offer not valid in Quebec. Credit or debit balances in a customer's account(s) may be offset by any other outstanding balance owed by or to the customer. Please allow 4 to 6 weeks for delivery. Offer available while quantities last. All orders subject to credit approval. Books received may not be as shown.

▼ If offer card is missing write to: The Reader Service, P.O. Box 1867, Buffalo, NY 14240-1867 or visit www.ReaderService.com ▼

NO POSTAGE
NECESSARY
IF MAILED
IN THE
UNITED STATES

BUSINESS REPLY MAIL
FIRST-CLASS MAIL   PERMIT NO. 717   BUFFALO, NY

POSTAGE WILL BE PAID BY ADDRESSEE

THE READER SERVICE
PO BOX 1867
BUFFALO NY 14240-9952

"Oh!" She grabbed her thighs. "Ouch!"

She attempted to stand but didn't have the strength in her arms to push herself off the bed.

"Ouch!" It was no use. She couldn't stand upright. Every muscle burned.

"I expected as much." Mable walked in and helped her off the bed. "I'll start you a nice hot bath so you can soak for a bit."

She led Miranda to the bathroom and turned on the faucets in the claw-foot tub.

"It happens to the best of them, child. I knew you would be sore today."

"I don't think a bath is such a good idea." Miranda braced herself on the sink to keep from falling. "Once I get in that thing, I won't be able to get out. I'll take a shower."

Even then, she wasn't quite sure how she would manage to swing her legs over the high sides of the tub.

"Are you sure?" Mable asked, getting her a clean towel. "A hot bath will do you a world of good."

"I'm sure. Afterward, I'll stretch and it should limber me right up."

Mable gave her some privacy. Muscles she never knew she had radiated pain when she moved. Heck, it hurt even when she breathed. She eyed the tub again as she gingerly pulled her T-shirt over her head. *Give me strength.*

JESSE SAT IN THE KITCHEN with a piping-hot cup of coffee in hand. Mable extended an open invitation to breakfast and whenever the mood struck him, he took her up on the offer. Today was just such a day. The aroma of fresh bread made his stomach stand up and take notice. A chef he wasn't and no one could beat Mable's breakfasts.

He feigned concern when Mable told him Miranda would be a few minutes longer due to her aching muscles. He could only imagine how sore she must be. But that was exactly how he wanted her to feel. Sore enough to realize this isn't her style of living and go home.

Mable cracked open fresh eggs from the henhouse and whisked them into an iron skillet. After all these years, she refused to use a nonstick pan. They were cheap and poorly made, in her opinion. In another skillet, she tossed slices of bacon. They immediately sizzled and the aroma permeated the air. He hated to admit it, but Mable's cooking even outdid his own mother's, although you would never hear him utter those words aloud.

Mable served him up a plate and joined him at the table, cup of coffee in hand. Much to his surprise, he found himself bragging about how well Miranda did yesterday in between bites of food.

He told Mable about moving the cattle to the north pasture. He wasn't planning to take Miranda, but now he rethought the idea. It would be a good experience for her.

"More like you are trying to scare the girl plumb off this ranch," Mable chided. "I have news for you, mister. All you will succeed in doing is causing her to sell off every head of the cattle you call yours. She's not about to give up this place, Jesse. So if you care anything about that herd of yours, I suggest you rethink your plan."

He knew Mable was right, but he had to scare some sense into her and she feared the cattle. Then again, he wasn't sure how much sense she had after buying a ranch, sight unseen.

Miranda appeared in the doorway and hobbled to the table.

Oh, I can't resist.

"Good morning, sunshine." Jesse rocked his chair backward on two legs. "Aren't you a sight for sore eyes?"

Miranda sat down very carefully. Mable placed an oven-warmed plate of hot breakfast before her. After a cup of coffee, she fingered the two aspirin Mable had laid out next to her juice glass.

"Aspirin? How about a shot of tequila and some morphine?" Miranda grumbled.

Jesse couldn't help himself. He found her condition so comical he started to laugh. Miranda looked from Mable to Jesse and back again.

Mable shook her head. "You sure do have a sense of humor, child."

"Who's joking? I need something stronger than these." Miranda winced as she lifted the aspirin to her mouth.

"Lucky for you, most of your work is in the stables today," Jesse reassured her. "I'll be out moving cattle, so I won't be back for a while. I thought about taking you with me, but I think we'll save that for another time."

Relief swept over Miranda when she found out she wouldn't be riding today.

"Unless you care to join us?"

"Jesse." Mable waved a spatula in Jesse's direction.

"I'm kidding, Mable."

"You're going to trust me with the horses all by my lonesome?" Smug as she was, Miranda was terrified to have that much responsibility where they were concerned.

"There are only a few horses staying behind and I already turned them out. My best cutters in training are coming with me."

Miranda forgot about the other riders. She assumed they went everywhere with their own horses in tow.

Jesse stood up and took a list out of his pocket. "This is what I need you to do today." He handed the list to Miranda. "Most of it you already know, some of it I will show you before I leave."

Miranda glanced at the novel he handed her. *Oh, he has to be kidding!*

"Is this a list for the month?"

"Oh, dear," Mable said as she cleared the dishes.

"Honey, it's what needs to be done today." Jesse grabbed his hat from the wall. "I'll meet you outside in five minutes."

Miranda laid her head on the table. "Heaven help me."

OUTSIDE JESSE GREETED his brother Cole, Aaron, Beau and Clay Tanner.

"Why don't you ride out and I'll catch up with you in a bit. I need to show Miranda a few things before I go."

"I bet you do, little brother," Cole teased. "Word around town is she's quite a looker."

Jesse gave his brother a playful shove. "She's a handful and not in a good way."

The brothers were still joking with each other when Miranda appeared on the porch. Cole let out a long wolf whistle.

"That is one fine-looking woman you got there, bro."

"Cut it out, Cole." Jesse watched as Miranda attempted to make a very bowlegged attempt down the stairs. "The woman hates me."

"Hey, Jesse, what did you do to the little woman last night?" Clay called out from the stables. Everyone joined in on his amusement.

"Oh, didn't he tell you?" Miranda said flatly. "He ravaged me. Which is why I'm walking all funny today."

The men roared. At least everyone except Jesse.

"Go on. Get out of here, will you?" Jesse shooed them away with his hat.

"Now you've gone and got them all riled up." Jesse motioned for Miranda to follow him.

"If they get turned on by an exhausted cripple, more power to them."

Miranda hobbled over to a long steel cooker on the back of a trailer and inhaled the scent.

"Beau towed it in. Mable's making barbeque for tonight."

Jesse explained how to use saddle soap and showed her where all the leather was to be cleaned and conditioned. She knew how to do most everything else on the list. He felt he was more than fair with the chores he gave her. None of it was backbreaking work. While he wanted the ranch for himself, he didn't want to kill her in the process. Today would be an easy day for her. At least she would have a break from him.

Jesse went over the last of the instructions and rode off.

IF I HAD THE ENERGY TO CRY, I think I would. What have I gotten myself into?

Before she dove into the tasks of the day, she attempted to call Jonathan again. Annoyed he never tried to call her back yesterday or respond to her email, she punched his number into the keypad of the phone in the stable office.

"Hello."

Incredible! Stunned that he'd answered, she almost dropped the phone. "So, you'll answer the phone when a strange number appears on your caller ID, but not when my cell phone does. How convenient."

"Miranda?"

"Yes it's me, you twit! You set me up!"

"Listen, sweetheart. I'm late for a meeting. I'll catch up with you later. But whatever you do, don't give up the ranch."

Click.

Miranda slumped into the worn leather chair behind Jesse's desk. *I can't believe he hung up on me!* It was way past the question of *if* he set her up. It was *why* he set her up. And why was he adamant that she hold on to the ranch? There had to be an explanation. Judging by his duck and dodge tactics, it couldn't be a logical one. She knew it was pointless, but she attempted to call him again.

Voice mail.

She wasn't surprised. At this rate, she may never know his reasons. But she'd be damned if she would give up.

Miranda finished mucking stalls and fed the horses. While she still feared handling them on her own, she didn't have any problems. She spoke Jesse's instructions aloud as she haltered each one. It calmed her and she thought it would let the horses get used to her voice.

She also noticed Mable watching her from the porch in case something went awry.

Though she never made mention of it, Miranda suspected Mable knew her way around a horse or two.

It was hot. So hot, she wouldn't be surprised if the chickens started laying hard-boiled eggs. She changed into a tank top instead of a T-shirt, hoping it would offer some relief under the sweltering June sun. It didn't. She sweated her way through Jesse's list and finished the blasted thing by the time the sun was about to set.

She looked around the stables. Air-conditioning. Horses should have air-conditioning. She wondered how difficult it would be to retrofit the stables with a cooling system of some sort. Then again, it's not as if she was planning to keep any of them. They were Jesse's pride and joy but he trained them to sell them. Although Miranda couldn't imagine bonding with the animals only to let them go.

Every part of her ached. After denying herself a soak in the tub this morning, she would indulge tonight. Even though the aroma of Mable's barbeque made her salivate, her bath took precedence.

Exhausted, she settled into the hot water. The stiffness eased from her body as she thought about Jesse's bet. He was determined. She'd give him that much. However, it was all she would give him. How he expected to win was beyond her. Working the ranch for a month may not be the easiest thing in the world, but it wasn't enough to make her leave the only place she'd ever truly felt was home.

Miranda regretfully dragged herself from the tub. Once in her bedroom, she threw on a clean shirt and shorts. She sat on the edge of her bed and pulled on her socks. The last thing she wanted to do was go down and listen to Jesse make some wise remark about her day.

"WHERE'S MIRANDA?" JESSE scratched Max behind the ears as he watched Mable pull the pork. It was customary to have a big barbeque whenever other people helped out on the ranch. Jesse was anxious to hear how Miranda made out.

"She came in a few minutes before you arrived. She finished your list. At least it's what I think she mumbled. She wanted to get cleaned up before supper."

"I bet she had a thing or two to say after I left." Jesse could only imagine how much she had to say behind his back.

"Nope. Never said a word. Didn't even come in for lunch. Had to chase her down just to get some water into her."

What? Jesse didn't believe it. He thought for sure she would have given up at some point during the day. At least to bad-mouth him for a spell. He thought his list would intimidate her right back to the city. Apparently, she had no problem with it. Tomorrow he'd make it longer.

Throughout the day, his thoughts had settled on Miranda. No matter how much he'd tried to focus on his work, she would pop in and out of his head. More in, than out. It wasn't his style to be so heartless toward a woman, but she had something he wanted. *More than one thing.* He wouldn't stop until he got it.

She was an attractive woman. Too attractive for him to be caught up in his feelings for her. The safest thing for him to do was send her packing. The sooner the better. He already let his guard down too much yesterday.

He enjoyed teaching her to ride. She'd looked beautiful with her hair falling loosely behind her. A sense of peace seemed to wash over her as she sat atop her mount. Gone were the lines of frustration and worry on her forehead. Her arms relaxed, the reins loose in her hands. It was a look he would forever imprint in his mind. It was the only time he'd seen her carefree.

Ever since he first laid eyes on Miranda, it was as if she carried the weight of the world on her shoulders. With Lone Star, she was as free as a bird. Sure, she's in a little pain now but he was certain the more she rode, the more she would fall in love with it.

This was good and bad. Jesse always loved to share his passion for horses with anyone who would listen. When a tenderfoot finds the trust in themselves and the animal, a beautiful relationship begins. Nothing beat the feeling of riding across a wide-open field astride a powerful animal. He could only compare it to an eagle in flight.

The question remained. Did he really want Miranda to become addicted to the sense of freedom? He had seriously mixed emotions about all of this. He felt Miranda needed some happiness in her life. It was rare she smiled unless it followed something sarcastic that shot from her mouth. When she did smile, her eyes betrayed her. There was always a sense of sadness and longing behind them. While he wanted her to be happy, he didn't want her to be happy on his ranch.

The barbeque was ready and still no sign of Miranda. Curiosity got the best of him, and he took the kitchen stairs two at a time. The bedroom door was open a crack. He peeked in.

"Miranda?"

No answer.

But then he heard the sound of her steady, even breathing. There she was, sound asleep on her back, half on the bed, half off. She looked so sweet and almost childlike. One sock was on and the other still clutched in her hand. Jesse enjoyed the moment. She couldn't argue with him when she was asleep. He hated to be mean, but the only way he would win the bet was to play a little dirty. He closed the door all the way and pounded on it.

"Miranda!" he shouted. "Supper time. You awake in there?"

Jesse kept up the thunderous pounding until the door flew open. A splash of water hit his face and then the door slammed shut.

Jesse stared at it. Water dripped from his face and down his shirt. *I didn't see that one coming.* In the past, women had thrown an alcoholic beverage or two at him. This was the first time it was water. He opened the door and let himself in.

"Thanks, darlin'. I needed to clean up a bit. It was dusty out there today."

Miranda curled up on the bed, with her back to him. He stood near the edge and poked her with his finger.

"Get out of here! You're filthy!" she yelled as she rolled over. "I did what you wanted me to do. Now leave me alone."

"Sugar, you look like you've been ridden hard and put away wet."

Miranda grabbed a throw pillow and used it literally.

Jesse ducked. "Now, now." He swatted her rump as she turned her back on him once again. "Mable's worked hard on that barbeque down there. Plus, it's Friday night."

"Who cares?" Miranda said, her voice muffled by the pillow.

"I care." Jesse exaggerated the words. "Everyone's going down to Slater's Mill for some dancing."

"Have fun."

"Come on." Jesse tried to pull the pillow away from her. "Don't tell me you're going to wimp out and not go. Everyone in town will be there."

"Tell them I said hello."

"All right, but you're never going to make it in this town if you don't come out and dance with the rest of us."

If anything, that would get her attention. He knew how much she wanted to fit in. Sure enough, she turned over and faced him. "You really know what buttons to push, don't you?"

"Come on. Let's eat. I'll clean up and we'll head into town."

SLATER'S MILL WAS WALL-TO-WALL people, most in jeans and cowboy boots, women included. Others wore out-rageous square dancing outfits. Certainly not some-thing, you would find on the rack at Neiman Marcus. Miranda watched as they twirled around the pine floor with ease and grace. As complicated as the steps were, she thought it looked like fun.

Jesse spotted some friends across the room. The ca-sual way he took Miranda's hand and led her to their table seemed so natural it surprised him when he real-ized what he was doing.

"Miranda, this here is my cousin Brandon Slater and his wife, Vicki. My uncle owns this place."

"It's very nice to meet you," Vicki said.

She was a petite blonde with bright blue eyes in sharp contrast to her husband's brawny build, dark hair and dark eyes. Brandon stood and tipped his hat toward Miranda. Miranda saw a resemblance between the two cousins.

"I'd stand up, but as you can see—" she pointed to her very pregnant belly "—my feet are killing me today."

"When are you due?" Miranda asked as she took a seat.

"Another four weeks." She patted her front. "Brandon's more nervous than I am. I keep telling him it's the most natural thing in the world. Go figure. So, tell me about yourself. We've heard so much about you."

Miranda laughed. "I hope you don't believe everything you hear." Miranda shot a glance sideways at Jesse.

"Only the good things, I promise," Vicki reassured.

"How about a spin on the dance floor?" Brandon helped his wife up from the chair and spun her around perfectly, pregnant and all.

"Honey, my feet hurt. Later, I promise."

"One dance. I'll make it a quick one."

Vicki nodded and joined her husband on the dance floor. Brandon held her close, as if the rest of the place didn't exist.

"What are you having, sugar?" Jesse wrapped his arm around Miranda's shoulder.

Her skin prickled at his touch. Nice wasn't his usual method of operation around her. Miranda didn't bother to shrug him off. She wanted to see how this played out. There was an ulterior motive somewhere. For curiosity's sake, she allowed herself to nestle against him, enjoying his warmth.

"A beer's fine. Thanks. Something light."

Jesse playfully squeezed her shoulder before he sauntered over to the bar.

Miranda missed his touch as soon as it broke. A flashback of their kiss in the motel room came to mind. She felt heat rise to her cheeks and glanced down before anyone noticed.

"Well, aren't you the prettiest thing here?" Cole said, and he came up to Miranda. "My brother sure is the lucky one tonight."

Miranda blushed more. "Thank you. But I can assure you, your brother and I are not together."

"Well, in that case, dance with me, pretty lady." Cole took her by the hand and led her onto the dance floor. Everyone was in the midst of a line dance.

"I don't know how," Miranda said as she watched Cole step to the music.

"You're about to learn."

Miranda followed his lead and after a few faulty steps almost resulting in the loss of Cole's big toe, she had the hang of it.

Jesse watched her from the side of the dance floor. She smiled and waved while he gave her a round of applause. She was tired and sore, but she was enjoying herself.

When the song ended, she was out of breath. How in the world could people stay out there song after song? When she returned to the table, Jesse was nowhere in sight.

She sat down beside Vicki and listened to her explain who was who on the dance floor. Vicki was loaded with gossip and fast became the first female friend she had in town, next to Mable.

"Now, the one over there, popping out of her shirt." Vicki pointed to a short brunette in yellow three-inch heels and an ultrashort mini skirt. "She's Shannon Winters. But all the guys call her 'Radio Station,' because anyone can pick her up, especially at night."

Miranda choked on the beer Jesse had left for her.

"I'm not kidding." Vicki's face went serious.

Vicki didn't mince words and Miranda found it very refreshing. She listened as Vicki continued to fill her in on everyone in town. Her heart stopped when she looked up to see Jesse on the dance floor. His arms enveloped a stunning, auburn-haired centerfold. All laughter subsided as she watched Jesse hold the woman close and whisper in her ear.

"Now, there's Lexi Lawson." Vicki shifted in her seat. "She's Ramblewood's equine vet. If you haven't seen her out at your place yet, you will soon."

Miranda hadn't considered Jesse might be seeing someone. She assumed since he was leaving town, he wasn't involved. By the way he held her and whispered in her ear, they were about as intimate as two people could get with their clothes on.

"Are they—" The words stuck in Miranda's throat.

"Together?" Vicki asked as Miranda nodded. "If Lexi had her way they sure would be. Jesse's kept his distance all these years. His brother Shane, on the other hand, has chased after her for as long as I can remember. She likes a challenge. Shane's too easy for her."

"He doesn't seem to be keeping his distance right

now," Miranda said before she could stop herself. "Not that I care."

Vicki laughed. "Sure, you don't, honey. You always get this worked up when you see two people dancing close."

Miranda couldn't take her eyes off them. They made a handsome couple. There was no doubt about it. Something in the pit of her stomach felt as if it was about to turn over. Maybe the barbeque was getting to her.

"Relax. Lexi's a great vet. The ultimate professional. She happens to be very reckless when it comes to her personal life. Not Jesse's style."

That didn't help the situation any. What if she sweet-talked Jesse into a reckless roll in the hay?

Aaron stood before her, blocking her view of the dance floor.

"How about a dance?" Aaron held out his hand.

"She'd love to," Vicki offered then whispered in Miranda's ear, "And make Jesse jealous while you're at it."

Aaron led Miranda to the center of the dance floor. A slow Garth Brooks song played while she wrapped her arms around his neck.

"There's nothing going on between them, you know."

"So I've heard." Miranda watched Jesse and Lexi out of the corner of her eye. Aaron spun her around so her back was to them. Then he pulled her in closer.

They swayed to the music as she closed her eyes to keep from looking their way. She rested her head on the shoulder of the one man who made her feel at ease. Maybe he was the one she should be falling for. At least he cared about her. Only he felt more brotherly to her than romantic.

Aaron kissed the top of Miranda's head. A platonic

gesture she found most comforting. She sighed as he stroked her back.

"I know he's a little rough around the edges, but all in all, he is a pretty good guy."

"Funny you should say that." Miranda looked up at Aaron. "Considering his hatred toward you."

"Yeah and whenever he gets into trouble, I'm the first person he calls. Every time. Even before Cole. So pay no mind to what he says."

Miranda glanced around the dance floor. Still entwined in each other's arms, Jesse and Lexi continued to dance. It shouldn't bother her. She had no claim to him, but for some reason, her heart ached right now. She closed her eyes again, in an attempt to block him out of her mind.

JESSE WATCHED MIRANDA close her eyes and settle closer to Aaron. He was transported back ten years, to the night he lost Rebecca Thompson. When Aaron kissed Miranda's head, his heart missed a few beats.

"When do you want to breed Montana?" Lexi asked.

Jesse kept his gaze focused on Miranda and Aaron. Lexi pulled back to look at him.

"Earth to Jesse." She followed his eyes to see what he found so fascinating.

"I'm sorry, Lexi. What did you say?"

"Listen, if you want to dance with her, then go on over there and cut in."

"I don't want to dance with her." Lexi didn't look convinced. "I'm looking out for her."

"Sure you are," Lexi said. "Well, I don't think you need to worry. She's in very capable hands."

"That's what I'm afraid of." Jesse shook his head

to erase the images that came to mind. "What did you ask me before?"

"Montana. When do you want to breed her? She'll be in heat soon and you know how much a young filly wants to mate when she's in heat."

Jesse stopped dancing. He knew Lexi well enough to know she was fueling the fire on purpose. He also knew her feelings toward him. It would be easy to give in. Even though Shane took their father's side about his working on the ranch, he wasn't about to betray his brother and steal the only woman he ever loved.

Jesse stomped to the table with Lexi right on his heels.

"Admit it. You have it bad for her," Lexi said as she slid into the chair beside him.

Cole returned with another round of beers. "Who's he got it bad for? Miranda?"

"I don't have it bad for anyone!"

"The heck you don't," Lexi said.

Lexi filled Cole in on the details. Jesse snorted in disgust as Miranda and Aaron danced to another slow song. They were closer than any two people had a right to be. Jesse started to stand, his body rigid.

"Take it easy there," Cole said as he grabbed his brother's arm.

Why is this woman getting under my skin? He knew no matter how many times he questioned himself, the one simple fact remained. She *was* under his skin and there was no getting around it. He had to win this bet and get her out of his life for his own sanity.

He was torn between working her to death so she would give up the ranch and making life easy for her so she would stay...with him. But making her life easy wouldn't get him the Double Trouble. Now it appeared she made the decision for him. Aaron was her choice. He couldn't blame her, at this point. Jesse was anything but nice to her since the moment she'd arrived. In the back of his mind, he had brought her here tonight to change all of it.

Lexi excused herself and left Cole to deal with his brother. Typical Lexi, raise the heat in the room and then split.

"Why are you so worked up?" Cole asked. "She's just dancing with the guy. Like you were with Lexi."

"That's different." Jesse pulled at the condensation-soaked label on his beer bottle. "I grew up with Lexi. There's nothing between us."

"And you think there's something going on between Aaron and Miranda?" Cole laughed. "If you've got it this bad, then why don't you show her how you feel?"

"I can't get involved with her," Jesse said, eyes still fixed on Miranda. "I want my ranch back. If I fall for her, she stays and I'll lose Double Trouble."

"Unless you fall so hard you marry her."

Marriage? To Miranda? If he married her, the ranch would be half his.

"What's wrong? Racking your brain for a reason why you can't marry her?"

"Come now, Cole. I didn't think you could be this devious."

"Why shouldn't you marry her? You'll have your ranch. You'll have her. You can't lose. But you just might lose if there really is something going on with Aaron and he beats you to it."

Jesse never thought of Miranda marrying someday. Whomever she married would own the ranch. Cole's idea had possibilities. Strong possibilities. The last thing Jesse ever wanted was Aaron to gain control of Double Trouble. Jesse eyed his nemesis as he swayed to the music with his arms wrapped around Miranda.

"Uh-oh. I know that look." Cole stood and placed a firm hand on Jesse's shoulder. "Let's get out of here before you make a scene."

"I'm fine," Jesse snarled as he shrugged off his brother. "I'm not leaving her here with him."

The song ended and Aaron led Miranda off the dance floor to a nearby table. Jesse watched Aaron touch the small of Miranda's back as he ran through introductions. She let out a genuine hearty laugh. She was having a good time with Aaron.

Jesse stood, knocking his brother back a step. Cole was right. There was no reason not to marry her. It was the perfect solution to his problem and it would prevent Aaron from getting his hands on the ranch and Miranda. In a few long strides, he was at her side.

"You'll have to excuse us," Jesse interrupted, and took hold of Miranda's hand. "We need to be heading home. We have a wedding to plan."

"A wedding?" Miranda laughed at him and pulled from his grip. "What on earth are you talking about?"

"Come home with me, Miranda." Jesse ignored the people staring at him. "Come home with me and let's start a life together."

"Jesse," Miranda whispered. "Why are you doing this? Please don't embarrass me. Go home."

The two men locked on each other. Aaron pushed between them.

"You both look like a couple of peacocks with your

chests puffed out," Cole growled at both of them. "Now knock it off."

The music had stopped. All eyes focused on their table. Miranda looked around. He knew he had embarrassed her. Again.

Whispering rose among the crowd. Jesse heard someone repeat his words to someone else.

Aaron turned to Miranda. "I'll take you home."

"You're not taking her anywhere." Jesse attempted to get past his brother to stop them from leaving. "I know what you're up to!"

Cole pushed Jesse down in a chair so hard it knocked the wind out of him.

A crowd gathered as Aaron led Miranda out the door.

"Why don't you tie a bow around her and serve her to him on a silver platter?" Cole hissed. "You just blew any chance you ever had with Miranda."

Everyone still stared at him. How could he have been so stupid to propose to her in the middle of Slater's Mill? How could he have been so stupid to propose, period?

By the time they reached the parking lot, Miranda and Aaron were nowhere in sight.

Chapter Eight

Aaron dropped Miranda off at the ranch. She thanked him for the ride, but didn't feel up to talking about it any further. Jesse had proposed to her! Of course, it had to be a joke. Another way to embarrass her in front of the town.

It made sense. The reason why he was so eager to get her to Slater's Mill even though he knew how tired she was. The way he goaded her so he could humiliate her in front of everyone. It was like The Magpie incident all over again.

Inside, Miranda gave Mable a brief rundown of the events at Slater's Mill. Mable poured two cups of coffee and set them on the table.

"How do you feel about Jesse?" Mable asked. She put out two plates and a freshly made peach pie.

"For you, I'll censor myself and say he's a small domestic horselike mammal."

Mable laughed. "That he is, child. But how do you really feel about him?"

Miranda sighed. She didn't know. One minute he was bossy, the next he was sweet as— Miranda took a bite of pie.

"Oh, Mable, this is so incredible." She savored the bite, hoping this conversation would quickly end.

"Glad you like it because you're going to learn how to bake it for the Fourth of July picnic." Mable didn't wait for her to protest. "You know what I think? You both are too pigheaded to admit how you feel about one another."

"Pigheaded?"

"I've known Jesse his entire life. Never once has he acted this foolish over a woman, especially one he's only known for a few days." Mable waved her fork as she spoke. "You, I don't know very well. But it isn't too hard to figure out. I see how you look at him. And I see how he looks at you."

"He looks at me?" Miranda straightened her shoulders.

"Comin' and goin', child."

Miranda took another bite of pie, her lips curled on the edges. There was no way she could ever make a pie this good.

"Is that silly grin of yours over Jesse or my pie?"

"Both," Miranda managed through a mouthful of pie.

"Well, that grin isn't going to get you anywhere if you don't do something about him. Before you two end up hating each other."

"I'm not very good at relationships, Mable." Miranda rinsed her plate at the sink. "I can't commit to someone only to have them leave me."

"Who said he'd leave you?"

"He did. He made it clear he'd go to Abilene if he loses this bet. I plan on winning. So what does that tell you?"

"It tells me Jesse is trying to work you to death so

you'll give up." Miranda froze in place. "Don't you see it? If he scares you enough to think he's leaving, you'll panic about running the place alone and go home. He wants this ranch and he's not about to leave it."

"Then he'll make me leave if he wins. Either way, one of us goes." Miranda slumped against the counter. "I've moved too many times and lost too many people to have to start over again. This is my home."

"It's both of yours," Mable said. "The sooner you two realize it, the sooner you can get on with your lives. Together."

MIRANDA WAS IN THE STABLES at seven, but there was no sign of Jesse. She haltered Lone Star and led her out to the first corral. Always nervous with the first horse, her confidence gained as she continued to turn the others out. She pushed the wheelbarrow down the center aisle when the tack room door flew open. Jesse grabbed her and pulled her inside.

Jesse's mouth came down upon hers before she could speak. Urgent at first. He molded her against him. When she didn't try to push him away the kisses slowed. Lips barely touched as each kiss became more intimate. He supported the full weight of her body in his arms.

Jesse pulled back, far enough to bring a bouquet of wildflowers between them.

"A peace offering for the way I acted last night." His eyes softened when she looked up.

The scent of daises and lavender delighted her. "And the kiss? Was it part of the peace offering, too?"

"Mmm-hmm." Jesse drew her in close and kissed her again. "I don't want to fight with you, Miranda."

"No, you want me to give up the ranch." Miranda leaned back on her heels.

Jesse inhaled slowly as he perched on one of the saddle stands. He drew her toward him.

"I don't know where this is going." His grip tightened as he ran his thumbs over the top of her hands. "But I do know I can't seem to get you off of my mind. I don't know what the right thing to do is anymore."

"What got into you last night?"

"I would ask you the same question." He spun her around as if she were on the dance floor. With her back to him, he pulled her close again.

From behind, Jesse rested his chin on her shoulder. She folded her hands over his in front of her. While she wanted to savor his closeness, she knew better than to trust him.

She turned slightly toward him and whispered, "I saw you with Lexi."

Jesse laughed. Irritated, Miranda faced him, waiting for an explanation.

"Lexi and I are old friends. We were talking about breeding."

"I'm sure you were." Miranda tried to walk away, but he wouldn't release his hold on her.

"You and Aaron, though, that's another story altogether."

"Aaron's been a sweetheart to me. We danced, and he introduced me to some of his friends who gave me some great ideas about the picnic, by the way."

"He looked like he was after more than friendship."

Miranda raised one brow. "Jealous? How about explaining your proposal?"

"I'd marry you in a heartbeat, if you'd only say yes."

Miranda's mouth fell open. He held her face in his hands and gave her a closed-mouth kiss. He drew back and walked through the door without a second glance.

No longer feeling in control, Jesse kept his distance for the remainder of the day. His kiss went further than he'd planned. Needing to clear his head, he rode out, checked the cattle and made only the most urgent repairs on the sections of fence. He had to admit to himself that Miranda wasn't about to back down from this bet. There was no stopping her. She would win and he would be on his way. He had to marry her.

Sweat trailed down between his shoulder blades. Summer was only days away. He leaned against a fence post to take a swig of water.

"What the—" Jesse reached around and removed a sliver of wood from his jeans. He had to replace another post. Mesquite was inexpensive, but it rotted too fast.

By sundown, Jesse was uncharacteristically saddle sore when he rode to the stables. After he watered and fed General Lee, he felt the back of his jeans again. There didn't seem to be anything there, but he was sure there was still a piece of mesquite sticking into him.

With no one in sight, he dropped his jeans in the middle of the stall.

"I wish I had my camera so I could show this to our grandkids."

Jesse spun around almost tripping over the jeans pooled around his knees.

"This isn't what it looks like, Miranda," he said as he yanked his jeans up and winced. General Lee nudged him forward.

"Sure it isn't."

"No really, Miranda. I have a hunk of mesquite in my—well, in my backside, if you must know." *This is really embarrassing.*

Miranda hauled him out of the stall, struggling to control her laughter. "Come on, cowboy. Drop 'em."

Jesse hesitated and then lowered his jeans again. What did he have to lose at this point? Making a fool out of himself had become second nature. Between last night and then again earlier today, what difference would this make?

"Aw, you look so cute in your boxers. You skipped the boxer briefs this time, huh?" She squatted down for a better look. Her hands gently tugged at his shorts sending his mind in another direction completely. "Wow, you sure do have a hunk in there, don't you. Hold still. Let me see if I can get it out."

Jesse attempted to look over his shoulder to see what she was doing. She handled his body with the utmost care. Hands, soft and warm, tightened around his backside as she kneaded the mesquite to the surface.

"Grandkids, huh?"

"I was kidding, Jesse. Don't read into it."

"I'm not." Grandchildren. Now there was a thought. A thought he easily pictured. All he ever wanted was to start a family of his own on this ranch. To see his children and their children ride over the grounds. Only he never found the right woman to share his dream.

"Now, what do we have here?"

Miranda jumped, causing Jesse to stumble forward. He regained his balance and furrowed his brows at Miranda.

"Mable, this isn't what it looks like," Miranda managed to choke out through her laughter. "Jesse has a splinter and I'm trying to get it out."

"She's lying. Don't believe a word she says," Jesse said as he glanced down at Miranda's disbelieving face. "She wanted a little nooky and jerked my jeans right down."

Miranda swatted Jesse on the backside.

"Ouch!" He yelped like a wounded coyote.

"You can get that splinter out yourself." Miranda stomped out of the barn while Mable shook her head.

MIRANDA SNICKERED WHEN JESSE walked through the kitchen door. She helped Mable bring the roast chicken, fresh green beans and corn to the table.

"Jesse, grab the coleslaw from the fridge," Mable said as she poured iced tea into tall chilled glasses. She added a wedge of lemon to each one and carried them to the table.

Jesse gingerly eased into a chair as the women watched with curiosity.

"For your information, I got it out," Jesse grumbled. "No thanks to you two."

Miranda took a bite of chicken, closed her eyes and savored the taste.

"Mable, this is wonderful. I've never had cooking like yours in my entire life. You make everything taste so amazing."

Jesse grunted and nodded, too busy with his own meal to speak.

Mable smiled. "I'm sure your mama was a good cook."

"In all her years, I can't remember her ever preparing a meal." Miranda ran through all the mealtimes they ever shared together. They were few and far between. Mostly takeout or cereal. Never a home-cooked meal.

"I'm sorry. I didn't know." Mable patted her hand.

"Don't be. I'm fine. Still working through it, but I'm fine," Miranda said as she poked at her corn with her fork.

"What are you working through?" Jesse blurted, clueless to the conversation.

The look Mable shot him spoke volumes. He hung his head like a child. Miranda never experienced so much protectiveness as Mable gave her.

"It's okay, Mable," she reassured. "My mother died of cirrhosis of the liver a little over a year ago. Long story short, she drank herself to death."

Jesse put down his fork and watched her intently. He waited for her to continue. Maybe it was time to get it all out in the open. Well, not everything.

Miranda was never sure if her mother ever truly cared about her. The result of a one-night stand, she was a constant reminder of her mother's screwed-up life until the day she died. A child was a burden and Claire made sure Miranda knew it every day while she was growing up. When her mother became a full-blown alcoholic, she became the burden on her daughter.

Rehabilitation centers and Alcoholics Anonymous could only do so much when the person didn't want help. Claire had used her cirrhosis of the liver diagnosis as a free pass to drink herself into oblivion. When the doctor laid the liver transplant option on the table, she'd adamantly refused. Claire had enough of this world and wanted out of it the fastest way possible. All Miranda could do was watch her mother dig her own grave.

"My mother was the only family I had," Miranda

added. "I never knew my father. For the most part, neither did my mother. It's just me now."

A lone tear rolled down Miranda's cheek. She didn't mean for the last part to come out. But it was how she felt. Alone. She had no one. Now Mable had fast become the closest thing to a mother she ever knew. She wiped at her cheek and took another bite of chicken.

"This is so good."

Mable and Jesse exchanged looks. A silent understanding washed over the table. Miranda didn't want to reminisce further about a life she wanted to leave behind.

"We need to talk about hiring more help around here," Jesse said, taking the cue to change the subject. "We can turn a profit if we get this place back to what it once was. But we would need help."

Miranda nodded. "I agree." She wiped her hands on a napkin and braced herself for the storm about to rage. "That's why I've decided to hire Aaron."

"You what?" Jesse and Mable said in unison.

Miranda looked at them both. "What is so wrong with him?"

"Why Aaron of all people?" Jesse asked while Mable shook her head.

"Because I trust him and feel comfortable having him around," Miranda replied. "He knows this ranch and the animals. Besides, he's the first one you call when you need help."

"No, he's the one I call when all options have run out." Jesse went to stand, but Mable's hand on his kept him seated. "I don't think Aaron's the best choice."

"Then tell me who is." Miranda waited for a response. None came. "Exactly."

"Have you discussed this with Aaron yet?" Jesse asked through clenched teeth.

"No, but I'm sure it won't be a problem." Miranda was confident her friend would take her up on her offer. "I want Double Trouble to be a working ranch again, like you do."

"Really?" A look of surprise washed over Jesse.

"Yes, really." Miranda walked to the screen door and looked out over the grounds. "I want you to continue to do what you do best. Training the horses."

"How gracious of you." Mable shot Jesse another warning glare.

"I also want to plant some crops in a section of the south pasture and eventually open up a vegetable stand of some sort here, along with a collectable shop or maybe an antiques store. I had my heart set on a clothing boutique in town but I changed my mind. I'd rather open something here on the ranch. I know it might take a few years to actually turn a profit, but I think we have a chance."

"Miranda," Jesse said, joining her at the door, "I appreciate your ambition, but all of your ideas take money and plenty of extra hands. Not just Aaron's."

"Aaron is all I can afford," Miranda said. "And even that might be a stretch."

"Why does it have to be Aaron?"

"Why do you still hate him after something that happened ten years ago?"

"Because he's doing it again!" Jesse flew out the door and stomped off to the stables.

"What is his problem?"

Miranda turned to see Mable shaking her head.

"Just when I thought you two were on the right track, you messed it all up by bringing Aaron into this."

"With all due respect, I'm doing what you suggested. That Jesse and I work together. I'm offering him a chance to stay on the ranch. What is so wrong with hiring Aaron?"

"Child, for starters, he has a reputation with the ladies." Mable cleared the dishes from the table as she spoke. "And while Jesse respects him as a horseman, he doesn't want to be in competition with you for your affections."

"Aaron's past or present personal life is none of my concern." Miranda shrugged. "I know where I fit in. It's as his friend and only as a friend. Why should I care if Jesse has a problem with this?"

"This isn't the big city, Miranda. It's a small town. Here in Ramblewood, people care about each other's feelings and opinions. Especially when they live together."

Live together? There's a rumor in the making. "We don't live together," Miranda stressed. "He has the foreman's house, I have mine."

"Well, you might as well be when he lives only fifty feet from you."

"So what?"

"All right, time to lay it on the line," Mable said. "Have you paid him yet for the work he's done here?"

"I gave him the check from the sale of the horses."

"That's paying to feed those animals. Have you paid him anything else?"

"No, I—"

"No, you haven't. You haven't discussed it with him.

And it's fine because he's not complaining. He loves this place. He'd give his life for this land."

"I understand, but—"

"It's backbreaking work, every day," Mable interrupted. "But he gladly does it. It's in his blood. Now you want to bring in someone he can't stand. You need to respect how he feels about it."

"I understand," Miranda interjected. "But I also understand I need to do what's best for the ranch. And he needs to respect my intentions, as well."

What was wrong with everyone around here? Miranda figured they would have been happy to hear her plans to get the ranch running well again. She had so many other ideas she wanted to talk over with Jesse. Although she knew their time together was limited, she wanted his opinion. She hoped he would be so enthralled and proud of her, he'd want to stay.

Miranda looked for Jesse in the stables. She found him, kneeling on the floor, a stall door laid out before him.

"Can we talk for a minute?"

"A minute. I've got work to do and I'm sure you have something to do in the house."

"Jesse, what am I supposed to do here?" She lightly touched his arm so he would look at her. "You tell me if you win this bet, the ranch is yours and I'm gone. I won't let it happen. So when I win, you'll leave. Your decision, not mine. What choice do I have but to hire someone I feel comfortable being around? Did you expect me to hire a stranger?"

Jesse stood and kissed her softly on the mouth.

"I don't want to lose anything."

Miranda understood the underlying meaning of his

words. Not only did he want the ranch, he wanted her. What she couldn't figure out was why. Was it out of jealousy of Aaron or did he truly have feelings for her? After his impromptu proposal last night, she bet on jealousy and her being the easiest way to gain ownership of the ranch. If they were married, he would have everything he wanted.

She'd only known him for a week, but she couldn't deny her attraction to him. He was stubborn and obstinate. So was she. He loved Double Trouble and wanted to return it to what it once was. So did she. They shared so much in common, yet she didn't know if she could trust him.

Trust had always been an issue with her. Her mother was too irresponsible to ever trust. When Claire's illness set in, her mother relied on her for everything. Miranda was there for her one hundred percent. There was no thank you. No I love you. No nothing. Only demands. Knowing her mother wouldn't be around much longer, Miranda did all she could to make her comfortable. No matter how hurtful her mother's words were.

Despite the earlier problems she faced when she arrived, Ramblewood felt like home. Miranda needed a place to call home more than anything. The town was small and intimate, the complete opposite of Washington, D.C. She was becoming who she always wanted to be. A small town girl, living in wide-open spaces. Working hard and doing something meaningful with her day. Actually making a difference.

"Forgive me," Miranda said. "But I don't know how to trust you. I don't know how to trust anyone anymore."

Jesse wrapped his arms around her waist and pulled her close. "You will, in time."

He kissed her with more urgency. The heat from his lips crushed against hers as they parted for him. She felt wanted right now. It was a feeling she didn't want to lose. More than once this week she found herself admitting she needed this man before her. And she needed him in more than one way.

Chapter Nine

By the end of the following week, summer was in full swing. Miranda worked by Jesse's side every day. She'd even convinced him hiring Aaron was a good idea. He had turned out to be a godsend in the end.

It became apparent Aaron was only interested in Miranda as a friend. Aaron sought her advice on matters of the heart and she went to him for house renovation ideas. Jesse felt like a heel for thinking the worst of him all this time. He finally broke down and apologized to both of them for his actions at Slater's Mill the week before.

Double Trouble may have consumed Aaron's days, but his new girlfriend, Kiley West, occupied his nights. And with Aaron occupied, Jesse had more one-on-one time with Miranda. She had no plans to lose the bet and wasn't about to give up Double Trouble. He had to work fast if he planned to sweep Miranda off her feet in a few short weeks.

Miranda's riding skills improved each day. Jesse felt comfortable enough to allow her to saddle her own horse. After the one time she didn't double-check the cinch, she learned her lesson fast. He still couldn't get the image of Miranda, the saddle slipping sideways, and her landing on the ground out of his mind. She was stunned but amused. Luckily, she didn't get hurt. Graceful the woman was not.

Miranda continued to exceed each challenge he threw her way. She seemed to enjoy the hard work and by Thursday morning, she beat him to the stables.

At night, everyone pitched in and helped Miranda renovate the house. The living room was now a light café au lait color. Jesse and Aaron installed white bead board around the perimeter of the room to add more of the cozy charm she wanted. Miranda picked out a sofa and love seat at Mayfield's pre-Fourth of July sale and a bedroom suite for one of the spare bedrooms at another yard sale. He had to admit, she was thrifty. She managed to furnish the entire house in less than two weeks, without breaking the bank.

When Aaron wasn't working the ranch or out with Kiley, he was in the midst of constructing a magnificent bookcase to house Miranda's ever-growing collection of romance novels. She snatched them up by the dozen for a steal at yard sales. She said she never allowed herself to believe in romance before now. Jesse liked to think he had a little something to do with it.

"I'm heading to Slater's tonight if you care to join me," Jesse asked as he filled one of the water troughs.

"I'd love to. I need to go over some picnic details with Vicki," Miranda said.

"I have to admit, curiosity is getting the best of me. I should have stipulated you had to plan this party without help." Jesse laughed.

"Well, you didn't and I have a million ideas. All I'll tell you is this year it starts in the morning and runs all day."

True to tradition, all of Ramblewood was invited. Excitement spread from neighbor to neighbor while the townsfolk anxiously awaited the event. Jesse hoped the picnic would finally put to rest the rumors he'd started before Miranda came to town.

Miranda, with the help of Vicki's mother and friends, planned a surprise baby shower for her new friend. It was her way of saying thank you for not judging her as so many others in town had. No thanks to Jesse, of course.

At Slater's Mill that evening, Miranda blended in like a Ramblewood regular. A stranger would never have guessed she wasn't born and raised here. She had more of a relaxed aura in recent days. They joined friends at a table near the dance floor.

"Your plans for the picnic all sound so wonderful, Miranda." Vicki rubbed her belly. "I hope I can hold out long enough to make it."

"I thought you had a few more weeks to go."

"I do. I just feel different lately. Then again, I've never done this before. This could be normal for all I know. The doctor told me yesterday I still wasn't ready."

"You're still coming out to the ranch tomorrow afternoon, right?" Miranda questioned.

"Of course. We only have a week left to get everything ready."

Vicki refused to sit at home and let life pass her by. She feared she'd miss something good if she wasn't around. Pregnant or not, she was religiously at Slater's Mill every Friday night. With her high-spirited outlook on life, Jesse teased he wouldn't be at all surprised if she gave birth on the dance floor and then did a cheer afterward.

"I feel neglected." Jesse pulled Miranda to her feet. "Ready to take a spin with me on the dance floor, sugar?"

"Why, Mr. Langtry, I never thought you'd ask," Miranda replied in her best Southern accent as she batted her eyelashes.

Vicki leaned toward Aaron. "So, when do you think the wedding will take place?"

Aaron laughed. "At the rate they're goin', I'd say no later than fall."

"EVERYTHING IN PLACE for the baby shower tomorrow?" Jesse pulled Miranda closer.

"All set." Miranda beamed. "As long as Brandon doesn't catch on."

"I have it covered. I told him I needed some advice on expanding the business. He already has some ideas. Very good ones. We should really look into it."

"That's if you win the bet." Miranda swayed to the music. "I have my own plans, too. The magazine I'm reading says I need to turn the soil over soon in order to get it ready for next spring."

"Magazine, huh?" Jesse laughed. "We'll talk about fiction versus reality later. Brandon will love this joint baby shower idea of yours. He feels left out of the whole experience, as he puts it."

"I'm a firm believer a baby shower should involve the father. It's his child, too."

Those words were music to his ears. He watched Brandon's enthusiasm grow with each passing month. Jesse wasn't sure who was more excited, Vicki or Brandon, but he was certain when Miranda was carrying his child, he'd be there every step of the way. He laughed at the ease with which she fit into his thoughts. The more time he spent with Miranda, the more he wanted to marry her. And not just for the ranch.

"Something funny?"

"Have I ever told you how incredible you are?"

In the dim light of Slater's Mill, he could see a hint of red spreading to Miranda's cheeks. "Jesse" was all she whispered as she laid her head on his chest. It was all he needed...for now.

THE RANCH BUSTLED WITH activity the following afternoon. Miranda and Vicki's mother, Ethel, fixed the salads while Mable put the finishing touches on her chocolate chip pecan pies and peach cobblers.

Bridgett arrived with a helium tank and balloons along with an assortment of pastries from The Magpie. Kiley brought cartons of handmade shower favors, which almost fell to the ground when Aaron snuck up behind her and kissed her neck.

Jesse and Aaron offered valet parking so they could hide everyone's car behind the main barn. The guests began to arrive around noon followed shortly by the guests of honor.

"Surprise!" everyone shouted.

Vicki began to cry with Brandon not too far behind her. Their parents escorted them to two chairs on a small platform, decorated in pink and blue.

"I can't believe you did this!" Vicki said to Miranda. "I had no idea!"

"It was my pleasure." Miranda hugged her friend. "You can't have a baby without a baby shower, now can you?"

"Just think," Jesse whispered in her ear. "It could be us someday."

Before she could respond, he was gone. *Was that an offer?* They may have grown closer over the past week, but they hadn't shared anything more than a few kisses. At this rate, she'd be happy if he agreed not to leave at the end of their bet.

The party was a success. While Miranda and Vicki waved goodbye to the last of the guests, Jesse helped Brandon load the gifts in the truck. Mable drove her sister home and Miranda bustled about cleaning up.

"I don't know how to thank you, Miranda." Tears welled in Vicki's eyes. "This was all so…so…so thoughtful."

"Don't you start crying," Miranda said as she hugged her. "You'll get me started."

"Honey," Brandon called to his wife. "I'll be out back. We're going to take a look at one of the horses."

"Okay, dear."

"Sit down, leave all this to me," Miranda said as she pulled out a kitchen chair. "Let me fix you a nice cup of decaf."

Miranda took out her notebook of ideas she had for the Fourth of July picnic. Mable and Vicki filled her in on the traditional meals and activities but she wanted to add some new ideas to put her own spin on things.

"I think I covered everything," Miranda said as she poured more coffee.

"It sure looks—" Vicki winced and her hand flew to her belly. "Whoa."

"Are you okay?" Miranda rushed to her friend's side.

"Whew!" A look of relief washed over her. "I think

so. It took me off guard. I think it was all of the excitement. Either that or gas."

"Are you sure?" Miranda asked as she glanced at the clock on the wall.

"Sure." Vicki brushed it off. "Now, where were we? You're okay on food since everyone will bring a dish of some sort. And the boys are all fixing barbeque."

Miranda watched beads of sweat form on Vicki's brow. As she dampened a dish towel at the kitchen sink, she looked out the window for Jesse and Brandon.

"Okay." Vicki squirmed to try to get into a comfortable position. "This isn't fun anymore."

Miranda stepped out on the porch and yelled for Brandon at the top of her lungs. Panicked when no one appeared, she told Vicki she would be right back and sprinted across the yard to the stables. Aaron grabbed Miranda as she ran by, while Kiley appeared from one of the stalls, noticeably disheveled.

"Slow down. What's going on?"

"Where's Brandon?" She was panting.

"They saddled up and took off about ten minutes ago," Aaron replied. "What's wrong?"

"I think Vicki's in labor." Miranda wrung her hands.

"For heaven's sake and you left her alone?" Aaron turned Miranda around in the direction of the house. "Go back in the house and I'll ride out after them."

"I'll call an ambulance," Kiley said as she reached for her cell phone.

Miranda bolted through the kitchen door. Paper towels covered the floor.

"I'm so sorry, Miranda." Horrified her water broke, Vicki frantically mopped the floor with her foot on the towels, while she braced herself between the counter and a chair. "I had no idea."

Miranda ushered Vicki over to one of the chairs and helped her sit down.

"It's okay." Miranda laughed nervously. "But it seems Brandon and Jesse took a ride. Aaron is looking for them now."

"Of all the times… Oh!" Vicki stood up. "Oh, I don't think there's time. This baby's coming now!"

"Now?" Kiley shrieked from the doorway. "Right now?"

Vicki rattled off Brandon's cell phone number, saying she hoped he hadn't left it in the truck. The women looked at each other when a ringing sound came from outside. Well, it wasn't in the truck, but the porch was no better.

"Leave it to my absentminded husband," Vicki joked through gritted teeth.

"Maybe you should lie down," Miranda said, afraid the baby would fall out with the way Vicki was walking around the kitchen.

"I read walking helps aid the delivery process," Vicki said as she paced the floor.

"Well, stop aiding it!" Kiley shrieked. "Wait for the ambulance to get here."

"I think we should drive you to the hospital," Miranda said.

"Oh!" Vicki doubled over in pain. "There's no time."

"No time!"

Miranda gave Kiley a look that said "shut up" in no uncertain terms. With a scared pregnant woman about to give birth in her kitchen, she didn't need a crazed buxom blonde flipping out on top of it.

"Miranda," Vicki pleaded, "you have to deliver this baby."

"Me?" Now Miranda started to sweat. "I never birthed a thing in my life."

"And I have?"

Don't we need to boil water or something? Miranda ran through the episodes of *Maternity Ward* she had seen on The Learning Channel. They made it look so easy on TV. If only Jesse or Aaron were here. With all the calving and foaling they've done, they would be more help than she was right now.

"You'll do fine," Vicki reassured. "If Sally can do it, I know you can."

"Sally? Who the heck is Sally?"

"My…dog. She…had…puppies," Vicki said through Lamaze breaths. She braced herself between the arch of the living room and Miranda. "A few weeks ago… by herself with no trouble. We can, ow, do this. It's, ow, perfectly natural."

"Kiley, grab towels from the bathrooms upstairs and some sheets from the linen closet. How long does it take Mable to drive her sister home?" Mable always knew what to do in any given situation.

Miranda led Vicki to the living room. Upstairs they heard Kiley slam doors and drawers trying to find what she needed. Another contraction swept over Vicki.

Miranda looked at the kitchen clock. *Too close. They are too close together.*

"Where are those sheets?" she yelled to the ceiling above.

Loud footsteps bounded down the stairs.

"Here!"

Kiley tossed the sheets at Miranda as if they were

on fire. After they smacked her square in the face, Miranda shot her a look that would have killed most people on the spot. She began to spread them out on the couch when Vicki started to protest.

"I already made a mess out of your kitchen floor. I'm not about to ruin your new couch."

Miranda ordered Kiley to grab the shower curtain liner out of her bathroom so they could use it under the sheets. They lowered Vicki onto the couch as another contraction came. She squeezed the back of the couch as she let out a scream of agony.

What was taking the ambulance so long to get here? And where were the men?

"Now," she spoke through her Lamaze breathing. "It's happening now."

"Stand by with those towels!" Miranda yelled to Kiley.

"VICKI!" BRANDON SHOUTED as he burst through the screen door and slipped on the paper towels. Jesse and Aaron steadied him as Kiley motioned to them to keep it down. She led them to the living room, where Vicki held a tiny bundle in her arms.

"Meet your daughter." Vicki gazed at her husband with tear-filled eyes.

Brandon stood frozen, staring at his wife and new baby. It was as if someone glued his boots to the floorboards. Jesse and Aaron looked at each other, shrugged and nudged him forward. He knelt down beside his wife.

"I'm a mother?" he asked. Everyone laughed. "I mean, I'm a father?"

"Yes, dear." Vicki moved aside the towel so he had

a better look at his daughter. "Randi Lynn Slater, meet your daddy."

"She's so beautiful," Brandon said through his tears.

"I named her after you, Miranda Lynn Archer." Vicki turned to Miranda and smiled. "I hope you don't mind my shortening her first name to Randi. You brought her into this world."

Now it was Miranda's turn to cry. Her hands still shook from the delivery.

"You brought her into this world. All I did was catch her on the way out."

"I think it's a perfect name for a perfect little girl." Brandon kissed his wife. "You did good, sweetheart."

"Oh, well, thank you." Vicki laughed. "That's mighty nice of you to say."

Sirens sounded in the distance.

"Well, it's about time!" Kiley said. "Where were they? Stuck behind a tractor full of manure?"

The paramedics took both mother and baby to the hospital. Brandon thanked Miranda repeatedly on his way out. Kiley rambled a mile a minute as she told Aaron how Miranda delivered the baby. He ushered her out the door so Miranda and Jesse could be alone.

Miranda collapsed on the love seat. "Did what I think just happened, really happen?"

Jesse sat beside her and she laid her head on his shoulder. He ran his fingers through her hair as she closed her eyes.

"You were incredible today," Jesse said softly. "I didn't know you had it in you."

"You?" Miranda lifted her head. "I didn't know I had it in me, either."

"What on earth happened in here?" Mable stood between the kitchen and the living room. "Who was in the ambulance that flew out of here?"

"Vicki." Miranda smiled.

"And her daughter," Jesse added.

Mable's hands flew to her round cheeks. "You mean to tell me she had the baby...here?"

"Thanks to Miranda," Jesse boasted.

"You delivered a baby?" Mable laughed. "What do you know about birthin' babies?"

"Eh, nothing to it."

"You scare the horses with the sound of your voice. You probably scared the child right on out of her."

"So that's how you did it," Jesse teased.

"Get out of here, both of you." Miranda tried to rise from the love seat.

"Where do you think you're going?" Jesse pulled her back down.

"To take a bath."

Jesse smiled provocatively at her.

"Alone, Jesse."

He pouted and swatted her bottom as she stood. "I'll be here when you're finished."

"Mable, remind me to buy a new shower curtain liner," Miranda said from the stairs.

"What happened to the one I just bought?"

"I found another use for it."

MIRANDA TURNED THE WATER to hot and waited for the steam to build. She sat on the edge of the tub and reran the events of the past hour in her head.

She helped bring a new life into this world. Never had she been so scared and so happy at the same time.

It was amazing how two people could create a perfect little person.

Miranda ran her hand over her abdomen. Now she finally had a home. But, home to her always meant a husband and children. She had neither. While she had feelings for Jesse, she wasn't sure where they would lead in the future. Their bet was still on the table, and neither of them was about to give up.

The fear of his leaving for Abilene soon loomed overhead. There were no guarantees in life except death and taxes, her mother used to say. Miranda knew enough not to get her hopes too high.

After her bath, Miranda padded into her bedroom and found the coverlet and the sheets on the bed folded down. A bouquet of wildflowers sat in a mason jar on the bedside table. The windows were open, inviting the breeze to waft in.

Jesse wrapped his arms around her waist from behind.

"Do you like the flowers?"

"They're beautiful." Miranda turned in his arms to face him. "Thank you." She rose on her tiptoes to kiss him softly on the lips.

Jesse took her by the hand and led her to the bed. She stopped short. Fear swept through her. She wasn't ready for this.

"Relax," Jesse said as he eased her onto the bed. "I just want to hold you for a while. Nothing more."

Tension lifted from Miranda's body as Jesse ran his hands up and down her back. His fingers worked the knots in her shoulders and the stiffness from her neck. She swung her legs up on the bed and lay back, taking him with her.

Jesse held her close. She listened to his heartbeat and the rhythmic sound of his breathing. As she drifted into sleep, she could have sworn she heard him say, "Someday, it will be us starting a family."

Chapter Ten

Fourth of July morning the townsfolk began to arrive. Jesse scrambled fresh eggs in an iron skillet the size of Texas over the barbeque pit. In another skillet, he fried up a mess of bacon and sausage. Mable brought out stacks of homemade biscuits and a giant kettle of grits for everyone to dig in to.

Cole joked he felt like he was on a cattle drive, eating a chuck wagon breakfast. It was just the feeling Miranda hoped to convey. Traditionally the picnic didn't start until noon. This year, she wanted to start the festivities early so everyone could eat breakfast outside together. She wanted a warm atmosphere, and what better way than to fill everyone's bellies with a fresh, hot breakfast? Jesse and Miranda agreed to put their bet aside for one day.

By noon, Miranda found a moment to relax and enjoy the scene she had created. Everything from casseroles to cakes lined the red-and-white-checked tables. She secured the corner of each table with red, white and blue ribbons. Kiley placed salads in bowls of ice. No one arrived empty-handed.

In the center of each table, Miranda placed a pot of artificial bluebonnets, Indian paintbrushes and white verbena she'd picked up at the dollar store to create a Texas patriotic floral arrangement. Aaron hung a twenty-foot American flag on one side of the barn roof and on the other side, the Lone Star flag.

Old-timers told stories of how they used to move cattle up and down trails for weeks on end. She admired their tenacity and the freedom they must have felt as they slept outside at night and enjoyed nature all day. The concrete jungle had gotten the best of her over the years. It wasn't until now she realized what drew her to the ranch. The very scene played out before her. Community and family, together as one.

Miranda joined Charlie Slater and asked him about his new granddaughter. He told her how he ran out and bought new video and digital cameras to take pictures of the baby. The only problem was he couldn't figure out how to load the film into the camera. When Miranda explained he needed a computer in order to use the digital camera, he made note of it and said he would go out tomorrow and get one. She offered to help him set everything up when he was ready.

Miranda was about to get up from the table when Charlotte Hargrove sat down directly across from her.

"Good morning, Miranda."

"Good morning," Miranda said flatly.

"I wanted to say I'm sorry." She slid a small gold foil-wrapped box across the table. "For you. For the way I treated you at The Magpie a few weeks ago."

"It's forgotten." Miranda slid the box to Charlotte. "I can't accept your gift."

"Please, take it as a peace offering," Charlotte said. "Or if you rather I left, I would more than understand."

"I invited everyone in Ramblewood." She rose from

the table. "You are welcome to stay as long as you'd like."

"Please, Miranda." Charlotte placed the box in Miranda's hands and closed her fingers around it.

Miranda reluctantly opened the box to reveal a porcelain and silver hair comb. Her name painted on it with yellow roses entwining the letters.

"This is beautiful." Too beautiful? Miranda faced Charlotte, trying to figure out the woman's ulterior motive. "But you didn't need to do this."

"You've given Ramblewood a tremendous gift by carrying on the Carters' tradition of this picnic. It was the very least I could do."

"Thank you."

Miranda talked to Charlotte for a while and learned she had six children. Two sets of twins, no less. Miranda thought of how nice it must be to have twins. Two in one shot. Not bad for a day's work.

She watched everyone who arrived with children in tow. It wasn't an outrageous request. Just a few children running around her house to make it complete. She watched Jesse as he taught his second cousin how to catch a softball, Max catching the balls he missed. He would make a great father someday. He truly seemed to love kids.

Miranda excused herself as she helped Aaron with iced tea detail.

"What's the matter, sunshine?" Aaron asked, filling an empty glass. "You look all down in the mouth."

"Nothing's wrong," Miranda said, but she knew by the look on his face he didn't believe her. "All right. With all these kids running around, I feel like my biological clock is ticking away without me."

"Ah. I see." Aaron set down the pitcher. "You help deliver one baby and now you want one of your own. I understand."

"It's not quite like that. You're a man. Men don't have biological clocks. You can keep making babies until the day you die. I figured by the age of thirty I would have had all the children I was going to have. Well, thirty's less than a year away and even if I start now, it isn't going to happen."

"Your time will come." Aaron gave her a quick hug. "Just be patient."

JESSE WAS CLOSE ENOUGH to hear the conversation between Miranda and Aaron. He reached into his pocket to double-check that the box he had been carrying around for the past few days was still there. He left breakfast duty to Beau and asked Miranda to take a walk with him.

"I heard what you said back there." Jesse squeezed Miranda's hand.

"I said a lot of things," Miranda teased. "What would you be referring to?"

"About having children."

Seeing his own children run around the Double Trouble Ranch had always been his plans for the future. Now that he was certain Miranda wanted the same thing, this was the moment he had waited for his entire life.

"Oh." Miranda released his hand and started to walk more on an angle to put some distance between them. She made it clear she didn't want to discuss the matter further.

"It's okay, you know," Jesse said as he doubled his steps to rein her in.

"What is?"

"Miranda, stop." He took hold of her hands so she couldn't walk away. "You're not the only one who expected to have a family by now." Jesse started to bend at the knees, when she released his hands suddenly again.

"Why don't we talk about this later?" She motioned toward her guests. "I want to have fun today, not be brought down by what I don't have in life."

Not waiting for a response from him, she walked to one of the tables and struck up a conversation.

Jesse wouldn't let anything deter him. If now wasn't the right time to propose, tonight would be.

It took Jesse a while, but the more time he spent with Miranda, the more he realized this was where she belonged. She didn't have anything to return to even if she had decided to pack it in. The bet didn't matter to him anymore. The future, with Miranda by his side, was all he saw. The ranch was an afterthought at this point.

MIDAFTERNOON, MIRANDA BUZZED from table to table. People had surrounded her as if she were a movie star. They wanted to know who she knew in D.C. and if she ever met the president. Even he was surprised to hear she wasn't interested in politics.

A local band played next to the dance floor the men laid earlier and quickly filled with people of all ages. Just about everyone in Ramblewood was there. Some out of friendship, but most out of curiosity about the new woman in their small town. Miranda delighted them all.

Children gathered around Miranda as she sat under an oak tree and read them Mother Goose stories. They begged her for more each time she reached the end of another story. She didn't seem to mind, and read until the children either fell asleep or wandered off in search of a new adventure.

Jesse and Cole turned one of the corrals into a make-shift rodeo ring, while Aaron gave horseback rides to children of all ages. Old tin washtubs packed with ice overflowed with bottled beer and soda.

Everyone took their turn on the dance floor in the setting sun. Miranda mastered the tush push and the Texas two-step, and was in the midst of learning another new line dance. For the event she wore red cowboy boots, a faded denim skirt and a white eyelet off-the-shoulder top. She was patriotic to a T. But Jesse saw more than that. She was home.

Vicki, Brandon and little Randi Lynn stopped by for a brief visit. Vicki and the baby remained in the truck as Miranda peeked in the side window. The baby was the spitting image of her mother. Another Ramblewood High cheerleader in the making.

"I had to swing by and see how your party was going," Vicki gushed. "I wish we could stay, but a newborn and all."

"I understand." Miranda hugged her through the window. "I'm taking lots of pictures so I can show you everything later."

Brandon walked to the back of the truck and picked up two bloodhound puppies from a tall padded box.

"A gift," Brandon said as he handed the squiggly bunches of energy to Miranda. "No ranch is complete without a few hounds running around."

Miranda almost cried as she held the puppies in her arms. Max stood on his hind legs to sniff the newest members of Double Trouble. Miranda knelt down so he could have a better look at his new playmates. Tail wagging, he checked each puppy over, making sure all parts were intact.

Vicki had tied red, white and blue ribbons on their collars, with bows the size of their heads. One was a red female and the other a black-and-tan male.

"I know the perfect names for these two," Miranda said as she placed the puppies on the grass. "Scarlett and Rhett."

Jesse rolled his eyes at her name choices, but then again, this was the same woman who needed an entire bookcase for her romance novels. Miranda rubbed their pudgy puppy bellies and they all laughed when the puppies tripped over their own feet.

"Brandon, honey," Vicki said through the window. "Hand Jesse that gift bag. Miranda's hands are full. Their food, shot records and a few toys are all in there. Call if you need anything."

"Vicki, this is so sweet of you." Miranda squealed when Rhett nibbled at her earring.

"I hope you think so a few days from now." Vicki laughed. "You told me you wanted children someday. Here's where you start. Welcome to mommyhood."

The ranch cleared out as everyone made their way down to Sparks Memorial Field for the fireworks display.

A few folks volunteered to stay behind to clean up and watch the horses. Jesse was usually one of them, but not this year. He wanted Miranda to see her first Texas Independence Day celebration with him by her side. With Mable's help, Jesse convinced her to leave the puppies with her and join him.

Since the fireworks tended to spook the horses when

they were in the corrals, Jesse moved them all inside
the stables and played country music throughout the
building. Aaron came up with the idea to dampen the
sound of the fireworks the week before. It was a good
one. Just another thing to add to Jesse's "reasons I am
such an ass" list.

JESSE AND MIRANDA FOLLOWED the trail of vehicles leaving the ranch. When everyone else headed toward the
field, Jesse made a sharp right turn onto a winding dirt
road that opened to Miller's pecan grove. He stopped
the truck on the top of a hill and turned off the engine.

"Wait here," he said as he hopped out of the truck.

Miranda heard his boots in the bed of the truck and
turned to see what he was doing.

"No peeking!" he shouted.

Miranda giggled and faced forward. He opened the
passenger-side door, took her by the hand and helped
her down. Around the back of the truck, the lowered
tailgate revealed blankets, bowls of fresh blueberries
and strawberries and a crock of whipped cream.

"And what kind of night do you have in mind, cowboy?" Miranda said with her hands on her hips.

"Not what you're thinking, sugar."

"I'm thinking I see whipped cream." Miranda dipped
her finger in the white fluff and licked it off. "It can
only mean one thing."

"Yep. It means I wanted to take you to the very spot
my folks took us kids to watch fireworks when we were
younger." He hopped onto the tailgate and helped her
up.

"And how many women have you brought up here
before?"

"Only you, sugar." Jesse patted a place beside him for her to sit. "To be honest, I had forgotten about this place until my brother brought it up the other day."

"This is really nice," she said as she settled against his arm. "I bet you and your family did a lot of things together when you were growing up."

"Yes and no. There's always a party or a celebration of some sort around here. Give Ramblewood a reason to get together and people will come. So yes, my family was always together, but it was never just us. It was the whole town."

Miranda pictured what it would have been like growing up in a small town. D.C. wasn't a bad place to live. It had the Smithsonian museums, which she visited more times than she could count, and concerts at the mall. The cherry blossoms in spring were breathtaking. But D.C. lacked the hometown warmth she was looking for, and she certainly never did any of those things with her mother. She learned early on to be independent.

It was hard to feel like you belonged in such a big city. You were just another face to the person you bumped into at the grocery store. In Ramblewood, you were a neighbor, a PTA member or the postmaster. You were someone who mattered. Someone whose name they all knew.

"If you look straight ahead—" Jesse pointed toward the valley below "—you'll see the fireworks come right up over there."

"I can't remember the last time I saw fireworks." Miranda reached for the bowl of strawberries. "I always took shifts on holidays, anything to get ahead."

"Did it work?"

"Are you kidding? All I managed to do was clock

more hours for the same lousy pay with no compensation whatsoever."

"Tell me something I don't already know about you," Jesse requested.

"Mmm. Okay." She hopped off the tailgate and turned to face him. A smile spread across her face. "I won your little side bet, Mr. Langtry. I pulled off an amazing Fourth of July picnic this town won't soon forget."

Jesse laughed while Miranda reached over her shoulder and patted herself on the back. While she danced in victory, he jumped down from the tailgate and applauded her. The vanilla scent of her hair permeated the air and he found it hard to control his desire to kiss her neck.

"Well done, sugar."

Miranda spun around and planted a kiss on his mouth. Fierce and deep with an urgency that wouldn't quit, taking Jesse by surprise. He did all but fall over to pull her closer.

Miranda shattered the kiss between them.

"That, Mr. Langtry, is what you'll be missing when I win our other bet."

"Oh, no, I'm not." He tugged her back to the truck and grabbed her hips. Her back pressed along the side of the truck, he ran his hands down her waist and around to her firm backside. A heat so intense made it nearly impossible to restrain himself any longer.

"Congratulations on the picnic—" Jesse squeezed her rump, lifting her off the ground "—but the rest of the bet isn't over yet. You forget, I'm one of the most successful horse trainers around. You're going to need me to keep that end of the business going."

Jesse kissed a trail across her collarbone. He lifted her skirt as his hands drifted up her outer thighs.

"If you're so successful then why couldn't you afford the ranch?" Miranda asked smugly. She regretted the words the instant they left her mouth.

Jesse released her, shook his head and jumped into the truck bed. The fruit and whipped cream became one as they flew into the cooler. He balled up the blankets and pushed them onto the bench seat, through the window.

"That was low," he spat. "Congratulations, sweetheart. I didn't think you had it in you."

Miranda watched in amazement as he packed up.

He slammed the tailgate. "You have five seconds to get in or I'm leaving you here."

"Jesse," she pleaded. "I'm sorry. I didn't mean it."

"Save it." He opened the driver's door. "And to think I thought there may be something between us. How could I be with someone who throws their money in my face?"

"I won the money in the Maryland Lottery."

"What?"

"I won the money." Miranda took a deep breath. "It was the one year anniversary of my mother's death. I bought a ticket at a gas station. And I won."

"I had no idea—"

"Oh, you had ideas. They were wrong, though." Miranda wanted everything out in the open. "I didn't rob a bank. I wasn't born with a silver spoon in my mouth. I wasn't always rich. And I'm still not rich. I didn't win millions and millions. I just won the stupid state lottery."

Jesse tried to pull her into his arms. "I wish you had

told me sooner. I wouldn't have jumped to so many wrong conclusions."

"How could I with you spouting off about earning a living?" She waved her hands in the air, brushing him away. "How you despised having things handed to you, like your family's ranch. How could I say Maryland handed me money and I didn't earn it? You would have lit into me more than you did when you assumed I was born into it."

"You're right. I would have." Jesse held out his hand to her. "Forgive me, Miranda. I was out of line so many times."

Miranda gazed out over the moonlit pecan grove. She wanted to go to him, curl up in his arms and stay there forever. No more arguments, no tension, no more bets. She wanted to trust him, only she didn't know how.

"Miranda?" He reached into the cab of the truck for the blankets and spread them out. "Please join me."

She silently climbed into the truck bed and settled against the back window.

"Let's try this again," Jesse said. "Tell me something about you I don't already know."

Miranda shrugged. "There isn't very much to tell."

"Sure there is. What were you like as a kid?"

Miranda straightened. Her childhood wasn't all unpleasant, just strange. And one she chose not to discuss with people. It was too painful since her mother's death. This time it was different. She wanted to share her life with Jesse. She wanted to let him in and tell him all of her hopes and dreams.

"My mom and I moved around a great deal when I was growing up." Miranda opened the cooler and took a handful of the berries and cream mixture. "Just when I made friends, we moved."

"I'm sorry," Jesse said.

"Don't be," Miranda was quick to add. "Every new place was an adventure to me. A constant fresh start."

"And it didn't bother you?"

"Not after a while. I learned to adjust. You know how when you're a kid and you get picked on at school, or you feel a teacher doesn't like you?"

Jesse nodded.

"Well, I never had to worry about it." She smiled. "I would make up all sorts of glamorous stories about where we had lived and why we moved. And my mom would always smile when I told her about them. I think she liked to believe the stories herself. We never moved far, just far enough to uproot my school and her job. When she had a job. Mostly we were running from evictions or everyone else she owed money to."

She leaned into Jesse's hand when he pushed a strand of her hair behind her ear. It felt good to get everything off her chest. She had tried to talk to Ethan about her childhood, but he was never interested. Jesse gave her his full attention, urging her to tell him more.

"I was usually one of the most popular kids in class." Miranda stretched out on the blanket as she continued. "If anything, it made me a stronger person."

"What do you want most out of life?" Jesse asked, playing with the hem of her shirt.

It was a question she hadn't expected, although an easy one to answer.

"Family," she whispered.

"Tell me again, sugar," he murmured as he pulled her on top of him.

"I want a family of my own. It's all I've ever wanted. I thought I would have one by now. But those dreams died months ago. It was why I came here."

A lone tear spilled onto her cheek. Jesse's lips slowly followed its path. He turned her mouth toward his and deepened the kiss.

"Tell me what you want, Jesse," Miranda whispered.

"The same thing you do." Jesse kissed her again. "It's the only reason I didn't stay at Bridle Dance with my brothers. I want my own family. My own legacy. I never found the right woman. I never found you."

His roughhewn hands glided across her skin. Their strength excited her. Her breath quickened with each kiss as he rolled her onto her back.

"Do you want me, Miranda?"

"Yes." The word escaped her lips.

"I need you." He eased her shirt over her head, kissing his way along her belly, to her bare breasts. "This has gone way past want. End this bet. Start a new legacy with me. Tonight. Right here."

His mouth came down upon hers before she could answer. The heat between their bodies grew, as did their need to become one. She gripped his arms, his muscles hard and tight.

"You are so beautiful." The huskiness in his voice alone sent Miranda dangerously near the edge. Jesse lifted her hips, sliding her skirt past them. "So very beautiful."

The moonlit sky began to burst forth with color, while Jesse and Miranda created fireworks of their own.

Chapter Eleven

Miranda bolted upright. The sun was on the horizon and they were still in the bed of Jesse's pickup. She studied the man beside her. His dark hair fell across his forehead. It wasn't often she saw him without his hat. The blankets fell dangerously low on his torso, almost revealing the pleasure she had experienced the night before.

She couldn't remember the fireworks in the sky. Then she remembered the one thing she wished she hadn't. The bet. He still wanted Double Trouble. *If the cowboy thinks I'll give up that easily, he better hold on to his spurs.*

Miranda wasn't about to repeat past mistakes by getting too involved until she was certain Jesse truly wanted to be with her for herself and not because he wanted control of the ranch. With the bet ending this week, Miranda knew Double Trouble meant more to him than anything or anyone ever could.

Fumbling around for her clothes, trying not to wake the sleeping form beside her, she tugged on her boots and hopped down, almost slipping on the dew-covered grass in front of the pecan grove. Even the birds were still asleep. The flashlight from the front seat guided her way, the sun began to peek over the horizon. She glanced back one last time, to the man who made love to her throughout the night.

There was no longer any doubt in her mind. She loved him. Three weeks ago, she never imagined she would feel this way about anyone, let alone Jesse. He was mean and ornery to her the second her booted feet touched Texas soil. And he was determined to drive her away from what was rightfully hers. While she would be the first to admit there was an attraction to him the moment she arrived, she should have left it for what it was. A little roll in the hay every now and then never hurt anyone. Every woman needed the feel of a strong man once in a while. But to allow herself to fall in love with Jesse was another story altogether.

He would never change. From his stupid bet to his lame proposal at Slater's Mill, he was always after one thing. Last night he was after something else. A guarantee the ranch would be his. How could she have fallen for the "let's start a legacy of our own" line?

Miles away from home, Miranda set off toward town hoping the walk would help clear her head.

THE WARMTH OF THE MORNING sun roused Jesse. He reached quietly for his jeans and the box that was in his pocket. Now was the perfect time. Twenty-four hours earlier, his intentions were to propose so he could own the ranch. Now he wanted to propose because he was in love with Miranda. She'd worked her way into his heart just as she'd worked her way into the heart of Ramblewood. Double Trouble wouldn't be the same without her. Jesse rolled over to wrap his arms around the woman he loved. Only she wasn't there.

"Miranda," he called out.

No answer.

He tugged on his jeans and jumped over the side of the truck. The damp grass made him dance in place while he reached for his socks and boots.

Hopping on one foot, he called out for her again. As he jammed his foot into his other boot, he noticed the matted grass leading away from the truck.

"Miranda!"

He jumped in and started the engine. *She couldn't have gotten far.*

Boot tracks led him to the main road and then stopped. He thought he would have seen her by now. He glanced at the clock. Not knowing how long she had been gone, he didn't know where she could be. It would have taken her a half hour, at best, to make it out of the grove alone. Turning onto the main road, he figured he would catch up to her on the way to the ranch.

HER FEET ACHED BY THE TIME she reached The Magpie. The familiar bell sounded as she walked through the door. She said her hellos to everyone and listened to their thank-yous as she made her way to the counter.

"Give me the largest and strongest cup of black coffee you've got."

"Are you okay?" Bridgett asked.

"It's been a long night. One I'd rather forget."

"Why don't you clean up a little." Bridgett reached for her handbag under the counter and handed it to Miranda. "There's a hairbrush and some makeup in there."

"Thank you." Miranda made her way to the bathroom, afraid of what her reflection in the mirror might reveal.

Wonderful! I look like a hooker after a wild night!
Her clothes were on crooked, her hair disheveled. What
those people out there must think. She had the same
clothes on from yesterday!

"Miranda?" Bridgett knocked once on the bathroom
door and peeked in. "These should fit you. I always
carry a spare set in my car, just in case."

Some women understood the situation all too well.
Miranda gratefully accepted the clothes and made herself as presentable as possible.

French toast, bacon and a large cup of coffee awaited
her when she returned to the counter. Bridgett thought
of everything.

"Thanks." Miranda smiled weakly.

"Miranda!" Karen Johnson shrieked, almost causing Miranda to fall off her stool. Miranda didn't know
the woman well, but remembered her from yesterday.

Miranda glanced at Bridgett, who gave her a comforting pat on the hand.

"What a wonderful picnic you threw yesterday. We
had the most wonderful time! Everything was just so
wonderful!"

Bridgett giggled as Miranda attempted a sweet-as-
pie smile.

"I'm glad you had a *wonderful* time, Mrs. Johnson."

"Oh, please, dear. Call me Karen," she said as she
handed Bridgett the money for the check. "Well, I have
to run off. See you soon!"

"Isn't she wonderful?" Bridgett mocked.

Miranda began to explain last night while Bridgett
rested her elbows on the counter and listened. When she
gave Miranda the ol' be-quiet look followed by a head

nod toward the door, she braced for the worst. She followed Bridgett's eyes to the Magpie entrance.

"Aaron." Miranda breathed a sigh of relief.

"Why don't you two grab the booth over there? Aaron, honey, you want your regular?"

Aaron nodded and gave Miranda a questioning look.

"Have a seat," Miranda said. "I need to talk to you."

JESSE RAN THROUGH THE BACK door of the farmhouse. "Miranda!"

Up the kitchen stairs and through the bedrooms he continued to call her name. There was no sign of her.

"Mable!" Jesse shouted as he ran up Mable's front stairs and pounded on the door. "Mable! Have you seen Miranda?"

Mable opened the door a crack so the puppies wouldn't escape.

"Where's Miranda?" Jesse panted.

"I thought she was with you," Mable said. "Gimme a sec and let me finish getting dressed. I'm half-naked over here."

Jesse paced the entire length of the porch until she emerged from the cottage.

"Settle down and tell me what this is all about."

"She's gone!" Jesse yelled. "She got up at some point, got dressed and left."

"Got dressed?" Mable raised an eyebrow.

There was no time for him to explain. Mable knew all about the birds and the bees. He was sure she could put two and two together.

"I followed her tracks in the grass until I hit the road. I thought she would have come straight here."

"How far away were you?"

"Miller's pecan grove." Jesse took his hat off and swiped his hand through his hair.

"Are you sure you didn't pass her along the way?" Mable questioned. "That's quite a haul on foot."

"Of course I'm sure," Jesse snapped. "I'm sorry, Mable. I'm worried. Maybe she's lost somewhere. I'm going back out for her. If she shows up, keep her here!"

Jesse leaped from the porch to the ground. He spun the tires as he raced back out. He gripped the steering wheel until his knuckles turned white. *Where can she be?*

"HE ONLY WANTS THE RANCH, Aaron." Miranda pushed away her plate. She wasn't hungry. "He tried to get me to call off the bet last night."

"I don't think that's the reason, Miranda." Aaron patted her hand across the table. "It's all going to be okay."

"There's something I haven't told you." Miranda couldn't bring herself to look him in the eyes. "I'm in love with him."

Aaron laughed. "I know you are, honey." He smiled at Miranda's questioning gaze. "We all know you are."

Miranda looked around The Magpie. Had she really made a fool out of herself in front of the entire town again? Did everyone know she was in love with a man set on leaving her in a week's time?

Aaron gripped her hand tighter.

"This isn't the Miranda I know," Aaron said. "What happened to the 'take no prisoners' girl that barreled into town?"

He was right. Here she was, falling apart because she spent the night with Jesse. So what? It was the most pleasurable night of her life. What did it matter? She loved the man and he didn't love her. Who cares? She did, hence her problem. She cared too much.

If she was ever going to survive, she needed to get him out of her head. He'd be gone soon enough and that would be the end of it. It would hurt for a while, but she'd manage.

"I'll just avoid him for the next week."

"No, you'll face him head-on. Jesse's not as bad as you think he is. He has some mighty strong feelings for you, Miranda. When he asks why you left, tell him. Don't play games. Now, come on, let me drive you home. I've got work to do on that ranch of yours."

Aaron convinced Miranda to wait at the ranch for Jesse. She sat at the kitchen table, sipping a cup of coffee when the phone rang. Mable went to answer it.

"Hello?" Mable said. "No, I'm sorry. He's not here right now. May I take a message?"

Miranda gave her a questioning look.

"Okay. Will do." Mable hung up the phone and rung her hands.

"Who was that?" Miranda was almost afraid to ask.

Mable took a deep breath and released it before she spoke. "It was the owner of the ranch in Abilene. He wanted to confirm Jesse's arrival next week."

THERE WAS NO SIGN OF MIRANDA anywhere. After Jesse drove around the outskirts of town for an hour, he decided to check back at the house to see if she'd shown up.

Mable greeted him coolly in the doorway.

"She doesn't want to talk to you."

"What are you talking about?" He opened the screen

door but Mable blocked his path. "Mable, come on, let me in."

"I'm sorry, Jesse. Miranda made it perfectly clear she does not want to talk to you."

"Oh, for heaven's sake. Miranda!" Jesse shouted over Mable's shoulder.

Mable slammed the door and left him to stand alone on the porch. Jesse stepped down and called up to Miranda's window.

"I don't know what I did, but I wish you'd talk to me!"

MIRANDA DID HER BEST to avoid Jesse over the course of the next two days. No matter how he rearranged his schedule, she managed to stay a step ahead of him. Mable brought a plate of supper out to him the first night, but he wasn't hungry. He wasn't angry. He wasn't anything...without Miranda. He prodded Mable for answers. But she said they needed to work it out together. How could he when she wouldn't talk to him?

Thoughts of Miranda lying in the bed of his truck transported him back to the other night. Down came the walls and any pretense they'd once held. At least that's what he thought. The events played over in his mind. What had he done wrong?

Consumed with trying to win the bet, Jesse felt terrible he neglected to call the ranch in Abilene to turn down their offer. Yesterday he told them he would pass, although a small part of him regretted it now. The way things were going with Miranda, there would be nothing left to keep him on the ranch soon.

He reached in his pocket and pulled out the small box he continued to carry. The diamond ring nestled between two pillows of blue velvet reflected the morning sun.

There was no reason for him to remain on the Double Trouble. He could go back to Bridle Dance and make his family happy. It wasn't what he wanted, but he couldn't stay here any longer. The woman he loved shut him out of her life without as much as an explanation.

As he turned General Lee out in the pasture, he noticed Miranda watching him from the porch. She regarded him for a moment, and then hung her head when Aaron joined her.

If she wants to talk to me, she can come down here. I've made enough of an effort. Jesse led two more horses to the corral. When he walked in the stables, Miranda, Aaron and Mable were waiting for him.

What's this? Did it take three people to ask him to leave?

"Jesse." Miranda stepped forward. Her voice strained. "There's something I need to tell you."

"Why don't we all go in the house." Aaron shifted.

"Say what you have to say, Miranda." Jesse tapped his foot.

"I'm not sure how to tell you this, but—"

"But what?" Jesse snapped. "Spit it out already."

"Do you want me to tell him?" Mable asked. Miranda shook her head.

"Tell me what? What's gotten into you three? You act like someone died."

The three of them stood before him, sympathy registered in their faces. Mable touched his arm. Jesse stumbled and reached for the stall door to keep his balance. An overwhelming sense of dread turned over in his stomach.

"Who?" Jesse's heart pounded in his chest. "Who, dammit!"

"Your father," Miranda said.

The walls around him began to spin out of control. Aaron rushed to his side and led him to a bench. All oxygen escaped his body as he gasped for air.

He looked to Miranda for answers. She knelt down before him and placed her hands on his knees. *This isn't happening.* It had to be a dream. *A nightmare!* He'd wake up soon and it would all be over.

"He died in his sleep, last night," Miranda said softly. "I'm so sorry."

Cole appeared at the stable entrance, his eyes swollen and red. *No! It isn't true! It can't be true!*

"Please, tell me this is some sort of a sick joke," he cried. "Please, Cole!"

Cole pulled his brother into his arms, motioning everyone to leave them alone. They held each other as they wept for the man who raised them.

"I never got to end the feud, Cole." Jesse sobbed. "Pop died hating me."

"He didn't hate you, Jess. He may not have liked some of your choices, but he didn't hate you. The only reason he wanted you at Bridle Dance was because he loved you so much. He wanted to share his dream with you. With all of us."

"Mom?" Jesse asked. "How's Mom doing?"

"Not good." Cole was straight to the point. "Shane took off when he heard the news and no one's heard from him since. Chase is doing his best to keep it together for her sake. You need to be out there with the family. Aaron can take care of this place. We need you home."

"THAT WAS ONE OF THE HARDEST THINGS I ever had to do, outside of burying my mother."

"Joe was a fine man and a hard worker," Mable said. "Never saw that man lying down. He worked Bridle Dance ever since he was knee-high to a grasshopper. Grew up on that ranch, just like his boys."

"Jesse's going to need you now," Aaron said to Miranda. "Forget the other night and be there for him. He needs you."

Mable agreed but Miranda protested.

"I think I'd just aggravate him at this point. I seem to have that effect on him."

Miranda looked out the kitchen window toward the stables. She knew how Jesse felt. The loss of a parent, no matter how old, was never easy. Even harder when they never had the chance to make peace.

"They're gone," Miranda said as she watched Jesse and Cole drive away.

"Hand me one of those casserole dishes on top of the fridge, child," Mable said as she removed a bubbling dish from the oven. "The three of us will head over later. Those boys have some grieving to do."

"Mable, mind if I borrow Miranda for a bit?" Aaron asked. "Jesse won't be back for a while, if ever. We have our hands full."

The days of relying on Jesse were over. It was time for the baby bird to leave the nest and spread her wings. Aaron couldn't have spoken truer words. They did have their hands full and it was up to her to keep the ranch afloat. Her finances had dwindled rapidly with the addition of Mable and Aaron. Now their fate was in her hands.

Half of the money coming into the ranch for the cut-

ting horses went to Jesse. Miranda thought the arrangement the Carters worked out years ago was fair. But
right now his family came first and she couldn't rely
on Jesse to be around. The ranch had no other income.

While they all tossed around ideas for the ranch,
Aaron suggest they start boarding horses. They wouldn't
be rolling in money but it was a quick solution. It was
her turn to take the reins and this was her first official
business decision.

Miranda knew the guilt Jesse carried right now.
Knowing how much it meant to his father to have him
at the family ranch and the pain he'd felt when Jesse
had turned him down. It was enough to drive a wedge
between father and son. Now Jesse had to live with his
decisions.

Beau and Brandon stopped by and offered to help
with the ranch for however long she needed them. Kiley
and Bridgett helped Mable in the kitchen. By day's end,
they loaded their vehicles with food and headed for the
Langtrys' to pay their respects.

Miranda's mouth fell open at the sight of the sprawl-
ing Bridle Dance ranch. Exquisite, it put Double Trouble's white clapboard farmhouse to shame. Magnificent
pecan trees lined either side of the road as far as the eye
could see. White rail fences surrounded the property
and each corral. An enormous three-story log home
stood at the end of the road. Incredible was the un-
derstatement of the year. She didn't know Jesse came
from a wealthy family. Why anyone would ever want to
leave this place was beyond her, but she admired him
for wanting to make it on his own.

"Close your mouth, child," Mable said. "You're about
to start catching flies."

Miranda snapped her mouth shut but continued to survey the place with wide eyes as they drove around to the rear of the house.

"Quite a place isn't it?" Aaron asked.

"I'll say." Miranda peered around Mable to see a bull in one corral. Barrels were lined up in another.

"Cole, Shane and Chase are all rodeo champions," Aaron said. "They still actively compete, but Shane has a great reputation as a teacher."

Mable led them through the back door. Mrs. Langtry greeted her old friend with a hug as she started to cry.

"Mable, I am so glad you're here."

After she paid her respects to Jesse's mother, Miranda wandered through the house in search of Jesse. Light shone at the end of a long hallway near the kitchen. A lifetime of photos lined the richly paneled walls. Ornate bookcases and filing cabinets decorated the room Miranda assumed was Joe's office.

Jesse sat behind his father's grand walnut desk with a brandy snifter in hand. He swirled the amber liquid around the glass, then took a sip. A large bruise had formed along his jawline. Miranda was afraid to ask where it came from.

"How are you holding up?" Miranda kicked herself for such a stupid question. He just lost his father. She knew how he was holding up. He wasn't.

"How am I?" He motioned for her to have a seat over on the leather couch as he stood. "Let's see. When I got here, Chase almost threw me off the porch. Shane was nowhere to be found and when he did surface he clocked me one, right in the jaw for always letting my father down."

He joined Miranda on the couch and continued.

"After a few rounds with them and my uncle threatening to shoot us all, Shane calmed down some. Not much, though. Chase on the other hand verbally attacked me when his fists lost their punch."

"Jesse, I'm so sorry."

"I know you are, sugar." He rested his head on her shoulder. "I wasted so much time not wanting to be here and a part of the family that I lost sight of who I really am."

"You're who you've always been. A strong, independent man with plans for his own family. No one can fault you for your dreams, Jesse."

"At Cole's insistence, my brothers offered me a stake in the ranch again." Jesse took another sip of brandy.

"What did you decide?"

"I haven't given them my answer yet." Jesse laughed. "Heck, our bet's almost up anyway. You're not going anywhere and I'm going to need somewhere to live. As much as I hate to admit it, you did good, sugar. Real good. I didn't think you had it in you."

"What about Abilene?" Miranda asked, pushing aside his compliment.

"I told them no yesterday. I felt bad about it, too. I meant to call them sooner and plumb forgot."

Miranda swallowed the acid taste in her mouth. She ignored him for the past few days because she thought he'd used her. He had no intentions of leaving town.

"Why did you run out on me, Miranda?"

"Because I thought you were using me and after only one thing," she whispered.

"I asked you to start a family with me. How could you think I was using you?"

Because her defenses were up. Because she was stubborn and jumped to conclusions all her life. Because she never learned to let someone love her. Because he wanted the ranch. Now didn't seem like the time to remind him of that.

Either way, she knew the time they spent together had ended. Even Aaron made it clear to her. Jesse's family needed him. They offered him a chance to come home. It was the best place for him. He could mend fences with his brothers and they could heal as a family.

She would miss his company and the times they'd shared, but it wasn't as if he was on the other side of the country. Just the other side of town. There would be plenty of chances to see each other. Only not on a daily basis. At least she hoped there would be chances.

The man before her taught her more in one month than she'd learned in a lifetime. He made her feel needed, as if she made a difference to the ranch and the town. She would always be thankful for him no matter how miserable he was to her in the beginning.

"Miranda?"

"Hmm?"

"You didn't answer me. Why did you think I was using you?"

"We'll talk about it some other time." Miranda didn't think now was the time to have this conversation.

"I need to know. Please tell me."

"I thought all you wanted was the ranch. You asked me to end the bet. I felt used," Miranda admitted. "And after the ranch in Abilene called for you the morning after...the morning after the Fourth of July, what was I supposed to think?"

"How did you know they called?"

"I was there when Mable answered the phone."

"Mable left that part out when she gave me the message." Jesse shook his head.

"I asked her not to tell you," Miranda said. "I didn't want you to know I knew your plans."

"But they weren't my plans." Jesse drew her closer to him on the couch. "My plans were to start a family with you. The family we both want."

"I'm sorry about your father, Jesse." Miranda stood. "I know you came in here to be alone. So I'll be on my way."

"Miranda, wait." Jesse reached out to stop her. "Please don't leave yet. I could really use your strength right now."

Chapter Twelve

Mable stayed at Bridle Dance to help Kay Langtry and the rest of the family. Aaron drove Miranda home. Later, he offered to spend the night on the ranch but she turned him down.

"Thank you, but I can manage," she said. "Go on home. I can handle things here."

"Tell you what. You go on inside and let me finish up out here. We'll talk about it in a few. You don't look so good."

"Oh, gee, thanks." The truth of the matter was her head started to pound a few hours ago. "I'm just drained."

In the house, Miranda made herself a glass of chocolate milk and sat on the couch while the puppies wrestled each other in the center of the living room. She attempted to go over her finances but found her thoughts drifting to Jesse. She considered driving back out to the ranch, but the hour was late. They would probably be asleep.

A hot bath and a few lit candles did nothing to relax her. Miranda's headache worsened and the candles made her sneeze.

"This is crazy!" Miranda threw on a pair of jeans and

a T-shirt. On her way out, she stopped by the stables to tell Aaron where she would be. He said he'd stay and take care of things.

Miranda entered Bridle Dance, relieved to see lights on in most of the house. The cars that filled the grounds earlier were gone. Jesse appeared uncomfortable with so many people in the house offering their condolences. She hoped he was beginning to find some peace.

Miranda hesitated at the door. *Maybe this isn't a good idea.* She didn't know the Langtry family and didn't want to intrude.

Mable opened the door before she had a chance to decide. "I heard you pull in, child," she said as she led Miranda into the kitchen.

"How thoughtful of you to come back," Kay said. She gave Miranda an affectionate hug. "Jesse is in his father's office. He hasn't come out all evening."

Down the hallway, Miranda raised her hand to knock, and then decided to try the knob instead. The heavy door opened easily. Jesse still sat at his father's desk. He thumbed his way through a photo album. A stack about a foot high of other albums sat next to him on the desk.

He didn't look up as she entered the room.

"I had forgotten so many of the times we spent to-gether." He turned the page. "We were more of a family than I remembered. Look at this one here."

Miranda pulled a chair over to sit beside him. He pointed to a photograph of all four boys and his father standing in front of a lake, all holding fishing poles.

"This was the coldest fishing trip I can remember." Jesse ran his fingers over the image of his father. "Pop insisted we go anyway. Even though the weather forecast said rain for the week. We pitched tents when we got there but they collapsed during the night in all the rain and mud. We were a mess. And Mom was none too pleased when we piled into her brand-new station wagon to stay dry."

The corners of his mouth lifted upward.

"The next morning we went to the campground office and rented a cabin for the remainder of the week. The fire barely kept us warm, but we had fun. We fished all day, even in the rain. We'd come back soaked to the bone, but loaded down with a mess of fish to fry for supper. It was the worst and the best trip we all had together."

Their eyes met. He needed her comfort and she would rather be by his side than any other place on earth. Miranda took his rough, calloused hands in hers and held them to her chest. He kissed her, his lips barely grazing hers.

"I want to show you something," he said.

Jesse led her to the stables. He fumbled for the light switch as he opened a door. Gold and silver shimmered among the blue ribbons covering the walls. Enlarged photographs of each of the boys framed the room.

"This was Pop's trophy room." Jesse let go of Miranda's hand as he read off the events on some of the trophies. "He brought everyone here so he could show them what his sons had accomplished. Every award we ever won is in here."

"There are so many of them." Miranda walked the perimeter of the room. "Is this you?"

Jesse laughed. "That was my first rodeo."

"Rodeo? Mable told me you didn't—"

"I didn't stick with it like my brothers did. They all

went on to the big time while I was more interested in training and breed management."

Miranda nodded as she looked around. It was obvious how proud Joe Langtry had been of his boys. Jesse included.

"Everything had to be a family event. From the rodeo to running this place."

Miranda placed a hand on Jesse's shoulder.

"My brothers honored his wishes. I was too damn stubborn to be a part of it. I rejected my own family because I didn't want to be a part of someone else's legacy."

"Jesse, it's okay. I'm sure your father understood."

"All he wanted was for me to come home. To train and breed cutting horses here, on family land, instead of somewhere else. He never asked me to stop doing what I loved most. He asked me to do it with him. I said no. I always said no."

Jesse left the room and sat on the bench in the corridor. Miranda closed the door and sat beside him.

"I told him he was the stubborn one. Always had to have things his way. I'm exactly like him, you know. Stubborn as the day is long. Look at me now. Not only did I lose my own legacy, I lost my father, as well."

"He forgives you, Jesse." Miranda draped her arm around his shoulder. "You must know he forgives you."

"I need you tonight." He kissed her. "I need you."

MIRANDA SPENT HER DAYS at Double Trouble and her evenings at Bridle Dance, usually arriving home around midnight. She was exhausted but determined to be there for Jesse.

The morning of the funeral, the brothers called a

temporary truce, for their mother's sake. Miranda hoped it would lead to a permanent one. Jesse had decided to stay on at Bridle Dance, at least for the time being.

Jesse asked Miranda to stand by his side during the service. He needed someone to lean on and she agreed to be there for him. He opened up to her about his regrets over the years and how he only wanted to make his family proud by succeeding on his own. He thought success meant property. It wasn't until his father's death that he realized success meant being proud of who you are and where you come from. He never made the time to start meaningful relationships with anyone. His focus was always on Double Trouble.

The amount of people who attended the funeral service amazed Miranda. The entire town of Ramblewood didn't have this many people. The Magpie closed its doors that morning, as did every business in town. If Jesse ever questioned his support system, all he had to do was look around.

Is that Jonathan? Miranda tried to get a better view through the sea of people around her. The man disappeared. *I must be seeing things.* Jonathan would never have a reason to show his face around here. She couldn't even get him on the telephone. Unless you counted a convenient static-filled call. Either way, whoever the man was, he looked an awful lot like him.

Miranda continued to watch for the mystery man while she stood in line next to Jesse. One by one, everyone offered their condolences. At the beginning of the line, Kay embraced and thanked each person for coming.

"Jon, this is a surprise!" Kay squealed in delight.

"How sweet of you to come all this way. Joe told me he saw you a few months ago. Big-time lawyer now I hear."

Miranda turned to see the man Kay was talking to. Her breath caught in her throat when Jonathan gave Jesse's mother a hug. As he moved down the line, each brother gave him a warm friendly embrace, as well. They all promised to sit down and reminisce later tonight.

Reminisce? Reminisce about what?

When Jonathan stood before Jesse, Miranda gave him a questioning look.

"Jon, my man." Jesse shook hands and hugged his apparent old friend. "How long has it been? Fifteen years or so?"

Jon? When had he become Jon?

"It's been a long time." Jonathan avoided eye contact with Miranda. "I'm sorry about your father. He was one of the good people."

"Yes, he was." Jesse nodded. "So where are you living now?"

"Washington, D.C. I'm working for a law firm up there. Hoping to open my own practice one day."

"You'll have to excuse my rudeness." Jesse wrapped an arm around Miranda's waist. "This here is Miranda Archer. She's from D.C., too. Wouldn't it be funny if you two knew each other?"

Jonathan met her eyes and shook his head slightly, warning her not to let on their involvement. Confused, Miranda complied. While her friend had a lot of explaining to do, the reception line at a funeral was not the place.

"Yes, wouldn't it be funny if we knew each other?"

Jonathan shook her hand. "You have a beautiful woman here, Jess, a very beautiful woman."

Go ahead and lay it on thick. You can't dig your way out of this one, o' pal of mine.

"Easy there, friend," Jesse teased. "She's spoken for."

Miranda didn't say a word for fear of what might come out of her mouth before she could stop it. She still couldn't make the connection. Jonathan told her he was from San Antonio. Why the secrecy?

She also knew Jonathan had paid a visit to Texas, a few months ago, which was how he knew Double Trouble was up for sale. But he gave the impression he was driving through and saw a For Sale sign. Not once did he mention he personally knew anyone involved.

It made sense now why he wouldn't return her phone calls. He didn't want her to know he knew Jesse and his family. But why? What was he hiding?

After the funeral, Miranda tried to corner Jonathan for some answers. Only he was having no part of it. He mingled with everyone, caught up on old times. Who would have thought he was a master evader? Or that he had any old times to catch up on in Ramblewood?

Jonathan had one eye on her the entire time, counteracting each move she made. By evening, Miranda was beyond frustrated.

Outside, Vicki sat in an old rocking chair, holding her daughter. She beamed with delight when little pudgy hands reached for her face.

"I really need to start carrying my camera with me." Miranda joined her friend. "She looks more and more like you every day."

"Thank you. How is Jesse managing through all this?"

"He's hanging in there." Miranda watched him through the kitchen window, talking to Cole. "He's in the 'if I only had done more' stage."

"It was such a shock," Vicki said. "I can only imagine how he must feel."

Speaking of shock.

"Vicki, what do you know about Jon Reese?" Miranda hoped her friend wouldn't ask too many questions regarding her inquiry.

"Jon." Vicki closed her eyes and smiled. "He was my first kiss. I was nine. He was a much older man at twelve. He kissed me right in front of the movie theater."

Not only did Vicki know the man, she'd kissed him, too? This was all too much.

"What do you really know about him? Why did he leave town?"

"What's with the interest in Jon?" Vicki stopped rocking. "Your hands are full with Jesse."

Miranda had no other choice but to let her friend in on the situation. Vicki's eyes grew wide as she listened to Miranda recount the past three months. Including the part about the lottery. After Vicki swore not to tell another living soul, Miranda told her Jon was her best friend in D.C. Only, she knew him as Jonathan.

"Honey, all I can tell you is Jon wanted out of this town in the worst way," Vicki said. "When he was accepted to Harvard, it was his ticket out of here. None of us ever heard from him again. His parents moved to San Antonio after he graduated. So if he returned home to visit, we never saw him."

So that was it? Just a case of another small town boy wanting to make it in the big city. Miranda still thought there was much more to it. While Jonathan hadn't talked much about his childhood, he hadn't avoided it, either. He was close to his parents. What was missing?

Inside, Miranda was determined to find out the truth. After searching the house, she realized Jonathan saw his opportunity and ducked out the front door while she was with Vicki. Knowing she wouldn't get any more answers tonight, Miranda spent a few more hours with Jesse and then headed home.

The lights in the bunkhouse were out. Miranda figured either Aaron was asleep or he was entertaining Kiley. Either way, she was glad he offered to stay at the ranch for a while. Especially since Mable was staying with Kay. She offered him full use of the house, but he said he felt more comfortable out back.

Miranda picked up the phone and punched in Jonathan's cell phone number. It didn't even ring. Just went straight to voice mail. She hung up without leaving a message. What was the point? It was obvious he had something to hide and he wasn't sharing it anytime soon.

When Miranda crawled into bed, she felt physically and emotionally drained. Every joint ached and her head throbbed. Just what she needed. A summer cold when there was so much to do around the ranch.

She drifted off to sleep easily when the puppies let out a few high-pitched barks. She turned over and reached into their bed to soothe them. Then she heard the noise herself. There was a faint knock coming from downstairs.

Miranda opened the bedroom door a tiny bit so the puppies wouldn't scurry out. The knock was louder. She made her way downstairs without turning on the lights.

From the archway of the kitchen, she could make out a male figure standing on her back porch.

She reached for the phone. She dialed Aaron's cell number. Before she reached the last digit, the man knocked again, this time calling her name.

"Jonathan?" Miranda flicked on the kitchen light.

She grabbed a cast-iron skillet from the countertop as she opened the door.

"Whoa, now." Jonathan eyed the skillet in her hand. "I know you're mad and I have some explaining to do, but please, Miranda, put down the pan."

"It's a skillet, *Jon*. Folks in these parts cook with iron skillets instead of frying pans. But you wouldn't know anything about skillets, not being from these parts and all. Oh, wait a minute. You would know, wouldn't you?"

"Miranda—" Jonathan released her grip on the skillet and placed it outside on the porch, safely out of her reach "—we need to talk."

Miranda laughed so hard she started coughing. "Now you want to talk? Are you kidding me? You're damn right we're going to talk."

"May I?" Jonathan pointed to one of the kitchen chairs. Miranda nodded. He loosened his tie and sat at the table. Hands clasped before him, he took a breath and slowly exhaled as he looked around the room. The bags under his eyes silently spoke of his many sleepless nights. Miranda didn't think they were due to any pending court cases. He never let work get the best of him. This was personal.

"I didn't stumble upon Double Trouble," he began.

"But you sure got yourself in a whole heap of it," Miranda interrupted.

"I guess I deserve that." Jonathan stood and walked

toward the dining room. "You did an amazing job on the place. I heard you kept the Carter tradition and hosted the Fourth of July picnic."

"Pretty familiar with that particular picnic, aren't you?" Miranda sat rigid at the table. Arms folded across her chest.

Jonathan turned to face her and leaned against the archway.

"Yes, I know everyone in this town, give or take a few of the children."

"And you kept this from me because…?"

"Because I was asked to." Jonathan gazed at the floor. "Joe arranged all this."

"Joe? Jesse's father, Joe?" Miranda's eyes widened.

"The big man himself." He crossed one leg in front of the other and rocked back on his heels. "Joe wanted Jesse to come home to Bridle Dance. Having someone outbid his son was the only way it would happen."

"But it didn't happen!" Miranda raised her voice. "Up until a few days ago, he was heading to Abilene. And how was this plan of yours supposed to work?"

"No one ever figured Jesse would leave town." Jonathan jammed his hands in his pockets. "Jesse loves it here—"

"Yes, he does. And you tore what he loved away from him. Rather you had me do it! If you had left well enough alone, Jesse would own Double Trouble. His father would have had to accept it and maybe they would have made peace by now. Instead, you got right into the heart of a family matter and fouled the whole thing up. Jesse and his dad never resolved anything. How could you do something so careless?"

"He contacted me, not the other way around. He

made me an offer I couldn't refuse. But things didn't exactly go as planned."

"You mean Joe paid you to do this?" Miranda questioned.

"You know how much I want to open my own practice. Joe said he could make that possible." Jonathan said. "But when Jesse started to fall for you, we thought things would turn around and he would at least stay in town for you."

"What are you saying?" Miranda's hands flew in the air. "You had people reporting back to you about us?"

"I didn't." Jonathan held his hands up in front of him. "Joe did, yes. Only to the family."

"Was I bait?"

"What? No, Miranda, no." Jonathan reached out toward her shoulders, only to have her pull away. "You were never really part of the equation. Just a mutual beneficial means to an end. This house was a fresh start for you. This was your dream. You needed this. You buying this house was the only role you played. It ended there. Jesse was supposed to go home. End of story."

"Only it wasn't the end," Miranda hissed. "A man died. A family stayed at war because you had to play God."

"This wasn't my idea!" Jonathan shouted.

"You didn't have to agree to it!"

"And if I didn't, someone else would." Jonathan raised his chin. "Whoever bought this place could have thrown Jesse off the land in under a second. This place could have been torn down or sold off piece by piece. Then everything would be gone. I did you both a favor."

"Favor?" Miranda crossed the room in a few short strides and stood inches from Jonathan's face. "I took everything from the man I love. Now his father is dead without either one of them ever making peace. This could have all been avoided."

Miranda slowly stepped away from Jonathan. "Leave."

"Miranda—"

"I said leave."

Jonathan took a deep breath as he lowered his gaze. He squared his shoulders, inhaled sharply and walked toward the door. With her back to him, he said, "You'll understand all of this someday. Until then, I'm sorry."

Miranda shuddered as the door closed. Her new life tossed upside down just as her old life was. Nothing felt real anymore. How could she ever tell Jesse his father arranged for him to lose the ranch?

Chapter Thirteen

By sunrise, Miranda had a headache the size of Texas. When Mable came through the kitchen door, Miranda was already at the table with a bottle of aspirin and a glass of water.

"Oh, my, you look like you have a touch of the green apple nasties." Mable felt Miranda's forehead with the back of her hand. "You feel warm. You need to take to the bed and rest, child. You're running yourself ragged."

Miranda pushed the kitchen chair back. "No, what I need is to get my butt in gear around here. I have a ranch with lots of expenses and no income. And I need to figure out how to keep us afloat."

"Morning." The screen door bounced against the door frame causing Miranda to wince. "What happened to you?"

Mable and Aaron stood before her. Her two best friends—and their financial futures depended on her. She could easily sell off what little livestock she had and eliminate the need for either of them. It would be a means to an end. A month ago, that was an option. Her life would be free of complications or responsibilities. Now she couldn't imagine life without them.

"This ranch needs to turn a profit. I can't rely on

Jesse to pull us through anymore. This means we will probably lose the cutting horses. I have some ideas I want to run by the two of you."

They brainstormed over coffee. While everyone had some great ideas, the one person's opinion she valued most was missing. Jesse had his own family and problems to deal with. As far as she was concerned, their bet was over. No one lost. No one won. The circumstances had changed. She didn't expect Jesse to choose Double Trouble over his own family's ranch—they needed him more than she did. Guilt may rule his heart at the moment, but he was a family man through and through. He belonged on Bridle Dance.

She didn't know how Jesse would feel after he learned the truth about his father's and Jonathan's machinations, but she knew she had to tell him. She missed the brash cowboy who challenged her at every turn. She missed the feel of his arms around her and his lips on hers. He could tick her off at every turn, and then make her feel desired with a single glance.

In a month, she felt closer to the people she met in Ramblewood than she ever did to anyone in Washington D.C. Except for Jonathan and Ethan. Both men betrayed her. Ethan's true colors shined through when her mother died, and nearly blinded her when she won the lottery.

Jonathan's duplicity was so unexpected. He was the brother she never had. To think he was part of such an elaborate scheme was almost unfathomable to her. If he hadn't admitted it to her last night, she never would have believed it. Now he was one more player in the game of life.

If someone had told Miranda a few months ago that her daily activities would involve taking care of livestock, she would have declared them insane. In all honesty, she reveled in it. At the end of the day, she'd accomplished something tangible. She never had that experience in retail. Some days were a little trying but when evening set in and she looked out over her ranch, she felt good about herself.

Miranda worked with Aaron in the stalls before he rode out to check the cattle. The scent of hay and horse didn't help her headache. Miranda jammed the shovel into the pile of pellet bedding and tossed it into General Lee's stall. The horse stood cross-tied to the archway.

Miranda ran her hand up and down the horse's muzzle as she fed him some carrots she brought with her. He snorted softly in her hand as he eagerly chewed his treat. General Lee stomped his foot and pushed her shoulder.

"What is it? More carrot?"

General Lee kicked at the ground and tried to shake his head from side to side. "All right, let's turn you out for a while."

Miranda untied the horse and led him from the barn. Her breath escaped her quickly causing her to hang on to the corral gate as she closed it. She pinched the bridge of her nose and squeezed her eyes tight. Pushing her shoulders back, she inhaled deeply.

Breathe in, breathe out. Come on, Miranda, stay focused.

It was midmorning and the heat was already oppressive. She stripped down to her tank top and tied her work shirt around her waist. Bracing herself along the corral fence, she made her way to the stables.

"You're as stubborn as he is," Aaron said from one of the stalls. "Take a break before you fall down. Go inside the house and cool off. You're more work for me if I have to keep my eye on you every two seconds."

Miranda shook her head. "I'm okay. It's just hotter than I expected today, that's all. I'm not used to this heat."

Aaron handed Miranda a bottle of water. "Hydrate."

"Thanks." Miranda took a sip. "Don't get Mable all in a lather, either. I'm fine. And whatever you do, don't bother Jesse with any of this nonsense."

Aaron rubbed his neck. He took his hat from his head and shook it in her direction. "Only if you promise me not to overdo it."

"I promise."

There was no need to worry either one of them. She had a little summer cold and she would get over it soon enough.

Aaron kept his literal word. He called Vicki instead.

Midafternoon, Vicki phoned to see how she was feeling.

"Aaron has a big mouth you know."

"He cares about you, kiddo. Now tell me what's really going on. Did you ever get ahold of Jon?"

"More like he got ahold of me in the middle of the night."

Vicki clicked her tongue throughout the story. "I'd hate to be in your shoes when you tell Jesse. But none of this really surprises me. This is classic Joe, to the end."

"He's done this before?" Miranda's jaw dropped.

"Not to this extent, but he was a family man, Miranda. He was willing to do pretty much anything to bring his family together."

At Vicki's urging, Miranda made an appointment with Dr. Shelia Lindstrom the following day for a checkup. She gave her a clean bill of health except for the cold she had. Her temperature was slightly elevated and her throat was on the sore side. Her only recommendations were rest and for her to drink plenty of fluids.

By the time evening rolled around, she was exhausted. Mable left a plate of roast chicken, vegetables and corn bread in the fridge before she headed out to her weekly bridge game. Miranda picked at the food before returning the plate to the fridge. There was a note from Aaron on the table letting her know he had finished early and went out to meet Kiley at Slater's Mill.

Miranda climbed the stairs to shower before she headed over to Bridle Dance to see Jesse.

The sound of thunder echoed through the house. Rain started to fall as she closed the windows. Through the dining room window, Miranda saw the stable doors were wide-open. She jerked on her boots and ran outside. By the time she reached the stables, she was soaked through.

She ran around to the side of the stable and closed each of the stalls' outer doors. Inside she checked to make sure the horses were still calm. General Lee paced his stall, visibly irritated. She tried to rub his muzzle as he walked by, but he wouldn't stop long enough to let her soothe him.

Montana circled and kicked General Lee's adjoining stall wall. General Lee pinned his ears back against his head at the sound of Montana's antics. Miranda entered the stall and saw the source of Montana's fear. A snake slithered across the floor a few feet in front of them. Her pulse quickened. The snake coiled in defense. Montana pushed against Miranda. The mare's eyes wide and focused on the snake. She didn't have time to halter the horse. She grabbed the horse by the mane and started to move her into a different stall. Halfway through the stall door, Montana reared, knocking Miranda to the ground.

JESSE LISTENED TO THE RAIN FALL against the metal roof of the house. He knew Aaron was taking care of the ranch, but he wanted to check on things for himself.

It had been days since he'd been home. *Home.* There wasn't a fraction of doubt left inside him. Double Trouble was his home and Miranda belonged there with him. There were a million reasons why he should stay on his family's ranch. Only one why he shouldn't. The one reason was all he needed.

He called the ranch before he left but didn't get an answer. He tried Aaron's cell phone next, only to reach his voice mail instead. His stomach tightened as he pushed the truck through the driving rain.

"What the—" Jesse slammed on the brakes and skidded sideways to a halt. A horse froze at the sight of his headlights, and then bolted past the front of the truck.

"Montana!" Jesse shouted as he opened the truck door. The horse tried to run through a row of shrubs on the side of the road but was unable to clear them. Thunder rang through the air and the horse reared. Another truck pulled up behind him while Jesse grabbed a rope from the bed of his. Jesse waved his arms to get Aaron's attention.

Aaron bolted from the truck when he saw the horse.

"Rope her!" They needed to bring Montana down before she harmed herself. Lightning flashed in the sky, spooking the horse again. The men braced themselves for the sound of thunder. "I can't get close enough to her. I'll rope her first and then you."

Jesse threw the lasso as Montana ran by. Missing her, he signaled to Aaron as he quickly recoiled his rope. After a few unsuccessful tries, Jesse threw again and roped the mare. He tightened his grip as Montana fought the restraint and the rope cut into his bare hands.

"Aaron, now!"

Aaron threw the second rope over the horse and managed to bring Montana under some semblance of control.

"How did she get out here?" Jesse yelled at Aaron.

"She was in her stall when I left," Aaron said.

"What do you mean when you left?" Jesse shouted. "Miranda can't handle this place alone!"

"I wasn't gone long. I finished up and met Kiley at Slater's for a bite to eat. When it started to rain, I headed back to shut down the stables. The storm came up too fast."

"It doesn't explain how she got out here," Jesse said, looking around. "Where's Miranda?"

"She wasn't home when I left. She called and said she would be gone most of the day. She's probably there now. What are we going to do here? It's too far to walk her back in this rain."

"Do you think you can control her while I get the trailer?" Jesse said.

"Yeah," Aaron replied. "As long as you get back here fast."

Jesse jumped in his truck and sped down the road toward the ranch. Aaron must have left the stall door unlatched. It was the only way Montana could have broken loose.

Miranda's truck was beside the house. He backed

his rig up to the first horse trailer. As he stepped out to hitch it up, he looked at he stables.

"Miranda!" The stable doors were open and he could see Miranda on the floor in the center.

"Jesse," she said as she struggled to stand. "Montana escaped. I am so sorry."

"Aaron has her." Jesse guided Miranda to a hay bale. "Are you all right? Do you hurt anywhere? I'm calling an ambulance."

"Slow down, cowboy," Miranda said, attempting a smile. "I'm fine but I feel like I was shot out of a cannon and missed the net."

"If Aaron had been at the ranch like he was supposed to be, none of this would have happened."

"It wasn't his fault," Miranda said. "He went out to dinner with Kiley. He's entitled to have a life, Jesse. What are you doing here, anyway?"

Before Jesse could tell her his decision to be with her, Aaron rode Montana bareback through the stable entrance. After Aaron closed Montana's stall door, Jesse charged him, grabbing his shirt and slamming him into the doors.

"What the hell were you thinking leaving Miranda here by herself?" Jesse growled, inches from Aaron's face. "I trusted you to take care of her."

Miranda tried to reason with the two men, but neither one would loosen his hold on his nemesis.

"Jessup Thomas Langtry, you unhand Aaron right this instant." Jesse turned to see Mable standing in the center of the stable holding an umbrella as if she was about to club the two of them. Jesse immediately released his grip, but didn't back away.

"Now you get over there and keep your hands to

yourself. Come with me, child." Mable motioned to Miranda. "Let's get you inside and into some clean clothes."

Mable wrapped one arm around Miranda and popped open the umbrella with the other and led her out of the stables.

THE FOLLOWING MORNING Mable gave Miranda explicit instructions for her to stay off her feet and rest. Mable threatened to take drastic measures if she even heard the patter of Miranda's feet on the floor. The threat of no more home-cooked meals kept her in bed. She couldn't imagine life without Mable's cooking. She couldn't imagine life without Mable, for that matter.

Jesse knocked and poked his head in the door. She sat up in bed thumbing through a magazine while Scarlett and Rhett played with her toes through the bed covers.

Jesse bent over, kissed Miranda on the forehead as he produced a bouquet of wildflowers from behind him.

She inhaled their fragrant scent. "Mmm. My favorites." Rhett climbed over Scarlett to see Miranda's present.

Jesse laughed and cradled the puppy, rubbing his pink belly.

"I would have liked to have done this more proper," Jesse said, returning the puppy to the bed, "but, I'm never going to know when the right time is."

Miranda tilted her head sideways as he lowered his gaze.

"I know I'm not perfect," Jesse said and Miranda snickered when he looked up at her. "And I know I can be stubborn."

"Tell me something I don't already know." Miranda laughed but Jesse remained serious.

"I can't tell you it's going to be wonderful all the time. And I know there will be problems and arguments. I snore sometimes and my feet don't always smell pretty. I can be forgetful and downright ornery on occasion."

"Jesse, what is this all about?"

"What I'm trying to say is, I know I have my faults. But will you marry me anyway?" He opened up his hand to produce a white gold and diamond ring. "This was my grandmother's engagement ring."

Miranda stared at the ring in silence.

"Say something, please," Jesse pleaded.

"I'm sorry," Miranda said. "But, I can't."

Jesse jumped off the bed. "You're turning me down?"

"Jesse, please, let me explain." Miranda struggled to sit up straighter. "A few days ago you were ready to move off this ranch for good. Our little bet is officially over today and I'm still here. You told me yourself you had no place to live, when you knew damn well you had a place here. With me."

"You could have asked me to stay."

"What right did I have?" Miranda asked. "Your father just died. Your brothers asked you to take over Bridle Dance with them. It was your decision, not mine."

"I can't believe this. I pour my heart out to you and you turn me down."

"Because you don't love me, Jesse!"

Jesse stumbled back as if she'd smacked him. "Think whatever you want."

The door slammed behind him, causing the puppies to whimper in his wake. Miranda held them both close to her chest as she stared at the ring on the nightstand. If only he had proposed to her out of love, she would accept in a heartbeat.

She slid the ring on her finger and held it up as she admired it. Mable stood in the doorway.

"What did you do to him this time?" Mable demanded.

"I turned down his marriage proposal," Miranda said as she stared at the ring.

"Doesn't look like it to me." She walked over and grabbed Miranda's hand roughly. "Enlighten me, child."

Jesse's proposal was probably the most honest thing she ever heard come out of a man's mouth. She knew he cared about her. And she knew his soul was behind the words, but it was his heart she waited on. She refused to marry a man who didn't love her. No matter how much she loved him.

"He doesn't love me, Mable. His heart belongs to Double Trouble. Not me."

"Foolish woman." Mable shook her head as she walked out of the bedroom. "Foolish woman."

JESSE COULDN'T BELIEVE Miranda refused him. He practiced his proposal all morning. Then she shot him down without even thinking it over.

She said he didn't love her. How could she think that? He needed her in his life. He needed her by his side and he told her as much. Certainly, she must know how he felt about her by now.

When Cole asked him to ride out on a neighbor's cattle drive, he didn't need to think twice. Separation from Miranda was just what he needed right now. It would give him a chance to clear his head and figure out his next move. Only he didn't know if his next move would be toward Miranda again or in the opposite direction.

The men left in the morning and were in the hills by nightfall.

Jesse and Cole sat around the campfire and talked over supper. Within an hour, the rest of the men joined in on the conversation. They all told him to swallow his pride when he got home, and march over to Miranda's door and tell her how much he loved her.

After three days away from her, he was ready to go home. He rehearsed his words over and over again until Cole rode up alongside him and told him the cattle were going to start falling in love with him if he didn't cut out the *I love you*s.

They had a few breakaways but Jesse was proud of General Lee. He was his best horse. Instinctively, he knew which way to turn. That is until General Lee turned to cut a lead cow and Jesse miscalculated the direction.

He flew off his horse and landed with a thud. Cole immediately rode up behind him and corrected so the cattle wouldn't trample his brother.

Jesse arrived at Bridle Dance battered and bruised. X-rays proved everything was still intact, except for his ego.

"How badly do you want Miranda?" Cole asked.

The two conspired along with Chase, and for the first time in years, Jesse felt close to his family.

WHILE JESSE WAS GONE, Miranda realized she needed to explain herself and tell him the truth about Jonathan. Although Mable seriously doubted he would even look at her, let alone talk to her after the way she treated him. She'd said, "You don't go messin' with a man's pride and expect him to welcome you with open arms."

Someone knocked at the back door. Miranda crossed the room to answer it while Mable tried to see who it was through the window.

"Cole," she said. "This is a surprise. Come on in."

"Ma'am." He took his hat off and held it in his hand. "There's something I need to tell you."

"Oh, no." She reached out to steady herself on the kitchen counter. "Please tell me Jesse is okay. Please, Cole."

"He's all right, but there was an accident on the trail, and…" He hesitated a moment, gripping the brim of his hat. "He's pretty banged up and he's been asking for you."

"Dear Lord, this family does not need another tragedy." Mable ushered them both toward the door.

Tears welled in Miranda's eyes. She was grateful he was alive, but scared he was hurt to the point he was asking for her.

"How bad is he?" she asked.

"You need to come out to the ranch and see for yourself." Cole led her through the door.

"The ranch?" Mable questioned. "He's not at the hospital?"

Miranda bounded down the stairs after Cole.

"He was in for X-rays all night," Cole called over his shoulder. "We brought him home a few hours ago."

"Take me to him." Miranda hopped in Cole's truck.

Mable stood on the porch and watched as they drove off. She picked up the phone and dialed. "Kay, what are your boys up to?"

WHEN MIRANDA ARRIVED at Bridle Dance, Chase was sitting on the front porch with his head in his hands. Cole had to give his little brother credit. He played his role perfectly. Miranda gripped Cole's arm as they walked through the door. Even his mother appeared upset.

Cole led Miranda upstairs to his brother's room. He had to admit, his brother looked awful. A lot worse than he actually was.

"Oh, Jesse!" Miranda cried as she ran to him. He grimaced when she attempted to hug him. Cole didn't think it was acting on his part. His brother was mighty banged up.

"Miranda, I'm so glad you're here," Jesse said. "There's something I need to tell you."

"There's something I need to tell you, too."

"Please, Miranda, let me go first. This is important."

Tears stung Miranda's cheeks. She already began to fear the worst. Cole motioned to Jesse it was time to move this along before she collapsed altogether.

"Miranda, I love you more than life itself. Now, for the third time, will you marry me?"

"Yes, oh, yes! That's what I wanted to tell you. I love you, too!"

Jesse jumped out of bed. "Did you hear, everyone? She loves me. We're getting married!" He winced as he pulled her into his arms.

"Hey, wait a minute!" Miranda said as she turned toward the doorway. Cole, Chase, Jonathan and Kay fought to see over one another. "What's going on here? Jonathan?" Miranda looked from Jesse to Jonathan. Jonathan nodded.

"He told you?" Miranda asked Jesse.

"He told me everything. I don't blame you, or Jon or even Pops. Life's too short to pass blame on anyone."

"And all this, I thought you were hurt. You big fake." Miranda elbowed Jesse in the ribs, causing him to double over in pain.

"Miranda—" Cole rushed to Jesse's side "—he really is hurt. Just not as bad as we led you to believe."

"I think my bruised ribs just became broken ribs."

All color drained from Miranda's face. "Oh, Jesse, I'm so sorry."

Jesse took her in his arms and kissed her.

"Are you sure you want to marry me?" Jesse asked.

"Yes." Miranda gazed deep into his eyes. "I want to be your wife, now and forever."

* * * * *

COMING NEXT MONTH
from Harlequin® American Romance®

AVAILABLE APRIL 2, 2013

#1445 HIS CALLAHAN BRIDE'S BABY
Callahan Cowboys
Tina Leonard
Sweet and independent Taylor Waters won't accept Falcon Callahan's marriage proposal. But he's determined to win Diablo's best girl, even when the whole town puts him to the test!

#1446 HER COWBOY DILEMMA
Coffee Creek, Montana
C.J. Carmichael
Prodigal daughter Cassidy Lambert is home—temporarily—to help out at the family ranch. But seeing local vet Dan Farley again is making her question her decision to live in the big city.

#1447 NO ORDINARY COWBOY
Rodeo Rebels
Marin Thomas
Lucy Durango needs Tony Bravo to teach her how to ride bulls. Tony reluctantly agrees, and he'll do what he can to keep her safe. Even if her daddy warns him to stay away....

#1448 THE RANCHER AND THE VET
Fatherhood
Julie Benson
Reed Montgomery returns to the family ranch in Colorado to care for his fourteen-year-old niece, Jess. There Reed must face his difficult past, his cowboy roots and Avery McAlister, the girl he loved and left.

You can find more information on upcoming Harlequin® titles, free excerpts and more at www.Harlequin.com.

HARCNM0313

REQUEST YOUR FREE BOOKS!
2 FREE NOVELS PLUS 2 FREE GIFTS!

HARLEQUIN

American Romance®

LOVE, HOME & HAPPINESS

YES! Please send me 2 FREE Harlequin® American Romance® novels and my 2 FREE gifts (gifts are worth about $10). After receiving them, if I don't wish to receive any more books, I can return the shipping statement marked "cancel." If I don't cancel, I will receive 4 brand-new novels every month and be billed just $4.49 per book in the U.S. or $5.24 per book in Canada. That's a savings of at least 14% off the cover price! It's quite a bargain! Shipping and handling is just 50¢ per book in the U.S. and 75¢ per book in Canada.* I understand that accepting the 2 free books and gifts places me under no obligation to buy anything. I can always return a shipment and cancel at any time. Even if I never buy another book, the two free books and gifts are mine to keep forever.

154/354 HDN FVPK

Name _____ (PLEASE PRINT)

Address _____ Apt. #

City _____ State/Prov. _____ Zip/Postal Code

Signature (if under 18, a parent or guardian must sign)

Mail to the **Harlequin®** Reader Service:
IN U.S.A.: P.O. Box 1867, Buffalo, NY 14240-1867
IN CANADA: P.O. Box 609, Fort Erie, Ontario L2A 5X3

Want to try two free books from another line?
Call 1-800-873-8635 or visit www.ReaderService.com.

* Terms and prices subject to change without notice. Prices do not include applicable taxes. Sales tax applicable in N.Y. Canadian residents will be charged applicable taxes. Offer not valid in Quebec. This offer is limited to one order per household. Not valid for current subscribers to Harlequin American Romance books. All orders subject to credit approval. Credit or debit balances in a customer's account(s) may be offset by any other outstanding balance owed by or to the customer. Please allow 4 to 6 weeks for delivery. Offer available while quantities last.

Your Privacy—The Harlequin® Reader Service is committed to protecting your privacy. Our Privacy Policy is available online at www.ReaderService.com or upon request from the Harlequin Reader Service.

We make a portion of our mailing list available to reputable third parties that offer products we believe may interest you. If you prefer that we not exchange your name with third parties, or if you wish to clarify or modify your communication preferences, please visit us at www.ReaderService.com/consumerschoice or write to us at Harlequin Reader Service Preference Service, P.O. Box 9062, Buffalo, NY 14269. Include your complete name and address.

HARI3

The CALLAHAN COWBOY *series continues with*
Tina Leonard's HIS CALLAHAN BRIDE'S BABY.

Falcon has his work cut out for him trying to convince
Taylor to be his wife—but if his proposal doesn't work,
he'll lose his ranch land to his siblings!

Taylor Waters was one of Diablo's "best" girls. She had a
reputation for being wild at heart. Untamable. Men threw
themselves at her feet and she walked all over them with a
sweet-natured smile.

Falcon Chacon Callahan studied the well-built brunette
behind the counter of Banger's Bait and Tackle diner. He'd
talked the owner, Jillian, into selling him one last beer, even
though the diner usually closed at the stroke of midnight on
the weekends. It was his Saturday night off from Rancho
Diablo, and he hadn't wanted to do anything but relax and
consider what he was going to do with his life once his job
at the ranch was over.

Taylor was more of an immediate interest. She smiled
that cute pixie smile at him and Falcon sipped his beer, de-
ciding on a whim—some might call it a hunch—to toss his
heart into the Taylor tizzy. "I need a wife," he said.

"So I hear. So we all hear." She came and sat on the
bar stool next to him. "You'll get it figured out eventually,
Falcon."

"Marry me, Taylor."

"I know you're not drunk enough to propose, Falcon.
You're just crazy, like we've always heard." She smiled so
adorably, all of the sting fled her words. In fact, she was so
cute about her opinion that Falcon felt his chest expand.

"I leave crazy to my brothers. My sister is the wild and
crazy one. Me, I'm somewhere on the other side of the

HAREXP0413

spectrum." He leaned over and kissed her lightly on the lips. Falcon grinned. "What's your answer, cupcake?"

"You're not serious." Taylor shook her head. "I've known you for over a year. Of all the Callahans, you're the one the town's got odds on being last to the altar." She got up and sashayed to the register. His eyes followed her movements hungrily. "A girl would be a fool to fall for you, Falcon Callahan."

That did not sound like a *yes*.

But Falcon is a cowboy who always gets his way! Watch for his story coming in April 2013, only from Harlequin® American Romance®.

Copyright © 2013 Tina Leonard

HAREXP0413

HARLEQUIN®

American ★ *Romance*®

C.J. CARMICHAEL

brings readers another story from

COFFEE CREEK, *Montana*

Cassidy Lambert has dreams of a big-city life, but when an outbreak of strangles puts the family ranch under quarantine, she steps in to help before it spreads from the family's riding horses to the quarter horse breeding stock. With the chance to keep her daughter for a little longer, ranch matriarch Olive Lambert is seizing the opportunity to match her daughter with the local vet, Dan Farley.

Cassidy thinks she knows what she wants from life—but suddenly nothing feels right without Dan.

Her Cowboy Dilemma

**Available from Harlequin® American Romance®
April 2, 2013!**

www.Harlequin.com

HAR75450

HARLEQUIN®

American ★ Romance®

Another touching tale from

MARIN THOMAS

No Ordinary Cowboy

After the death of his best friend, border patrol agent
Tony Bravo needs a job transfer to San Diego to help
him move on and forget. Lucy Durango is making him
rethink his plans. With Tony's help, Lucy is determined
to make amends for her role in her brother's death
and hopes her efforts are enough to convince Tony to
forgive her. But she doesn't expect to learn that Tony
feels just as much guilt as she does, making her believe
that together they can find the peace they've both been
searching for and a future together.

RODEO REBELS

**Available from Harlequin® American Romance®
April 2, 2013!**

www.Harlequin.com

HAR75451